Clark remembe... Mrs. Wu complaining about how the house was always cold, which is why he chuckled when a massive oil truck rumbled past him.

I'd bet money that truck's heading for —

Clark inhaled sharply. Instead of slowing in front of Tina's house, the truck was bearing down directly on the home.

Did the driver pass out? If the truck hits the house . . .

But he had no time to think, no time to consider whether anyone would see what he was about to do. He churned his legs in an amazing burst of speed, going into Clark time. . . . Clark took a mighty leap up and through the driver's side window. Razor-sharp glass shards flew in all directions.

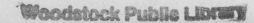

SMALLVILLE™

Available from Little, Brown and Company

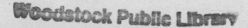

SMALLVILLE™

Speed

Cherie Bennett and Jeff Gottesfeld

Superman created by
Jerry Siegel and Joe Shuster

 LITTLE, BROWN AND COMPANY

New York ❧ An AOL Time Warner Company

For Steve Korté, keeper of the super hero flame

First Edition

The characters and events portrayed in this book are
fictitious. Any similarity to real persons, living or dead, is
coincidental and not intended by the author.

Library of Congress Cataloging-in-Publication Data

Bennett, Cherie.
    Speed / Cherie Bennett and Jeff Gottesfeld — 1st ed.
        p.   cm.
    "Superman created by Jerry Siegel and Joe Shuster."
    Summary: Teenage Clark Kent secretly uses his super-
powers to find the perpetrator of several racial hate
crimes in Smallville.
    ISBN 0-316-16816-5
    [1. Heroes — Fiction. 2. Hate crimes — Fiction.
3. Toleration — Fiction. 4. Mystery and detective
stories.] I. Gottesfeld, Jeff. II. Title.

PZ7.B43912 Sp 2003   2002035919
[Fic] — dc21

10 9 8 7 6 5 4 3 2 1

Q-BF

Printed in the United States of America

Chapter 1

"It looks great," Clark Kent said, peering over Lana Lang's shoulder at the stack of flyers she was holding. He and Lana had just parked in the student lot and were heading for Smallville High, where they planned to post the flyers in the hallways.

"It does, doesn't it?" Lana agreed. "Chloe told me she hit up someone on the *Torch* to design it. Whoever he is, he's a terrific artist."

They stopped for a moment to regard one of the flyers. It featured a cartoon border of children of every nationality, size, and shape; the kids were tumbling and dancing around a rainbow-colored ribbon. The center of the flyer read:

SMALLVILLE MULTICULTURAL DAY CELEBRATION
— Fun, food, crafts, and entertainment
to celebrate the diversity of Smallville—

Underneath the main heading were details about the town's multicultural festival slated for the following Sunday, including the time and place of various events.

"It's so cool that Smallville is doing this," Clark said as they continued on their way into the school. "How many small towns in America have a multicultural day?"

"Oh, probably as many as have a Lex Luthor available to underwrite it," Lana replied.

Clark laughed and held the front door for her; they entered the cool, fluorescent-lit corridor. School had let out an hour before. "Come on, Lana. You don't really believe that Lex is the only reason we're having this festival."

"I concede it's not the *only* reason," she allowed, pulling a roll of masking tape from the pocket of her jean jacket. She ripped off pieces and handed them to Clark, who began to tape flyers along the wall and on classroom doors. Principal Reynolds had given them permission to put the flyers up anywhere they wanted.

"Anyway," Lana continued, "I'm the last person to complain about Lex's generosity. If it wasn't for him underwriting my enterprise, I wouldn't be running the Talon." She handed Clark another piece of tape.

"Hey, it's not every teenage girl who's the boss of a restaurant," Clark teased, taping a flyer to the door of Mr. Ballister's room. He was their American History teacher, much loathed by their friend Pete Ross. Clark wasn't all that fond of him, either. Mr. Ballister had a volatile temper.

"That's just it," Lana said. "Because Lex owns the Talon, it's as if he owns me." She looked thoughtful for a moment. "I guess sometimes all the power he has kind of weirds me out. He seems to know everything about everyone, but I never really feel like I know the truth about him."

"Well, he's always been honest with me." Clark taped a flyer to the bulletin board outside the main office. Next to it was a trophy case filled

3

with sports trophies Smallville High teams had won over the years. Last year's trophy for their football team was prominently displayed. And engraved into the gold plating was the name of the team's most valuable player, Whitney Fordman.

Lana's boyfriend, Clark thought as he taped up another flyer. *Even though he enlisted in the Marines and he's far away from Smallville, it's like he's still with Lana all the time. I'm here, Whitney's not, and I still can't have her.*

"Whitney's trophy," Clark pointed out, hoping to sound casual. "The Crows missed him this season. Not as much as you do, though, I'm sure."

I'm just fishing to see what she'll say, Clark admitted to himself. *So I'm not perfect. I'm only hum —*

Clark had to stop his own train of thought because it almost made him laugh out loud. *I'm only human* is what he'd been thinking. Except that he wasn't human. He was from another planet, far, far away. As much as he was a part of Smallville, he could never fully belong the way everyone else could. It was a secret he could share only

4

with his adoptive parents, Jonathan and Martha Kent, and he'd have to live with it for the rest of his life.

He looked over at Lana, wondering what it would be like to tell her the truth. Would she fear him or loathe him? Her luminous face was reflected in the glass of the trophy case. She'd already experienced so much sorrow in her life, losing both of her parents when she was only three. But although the sadness was a part of her, it didn't define her, and Clark admired her for that.

I would do anything to make her happy.

Clark's feelings for Lana went way beyond the usual high school crush or passing romance. It was a connection, Clark was sure, that transcended time and space. He didn't have any words for it, but didn't really feel that he needed any. No matter where he was or what he was doing, Lana was always in his heart. And more and more often, he found himself thinking that she shared his feelings.

But then, there's Whitney. There's always Whitney.

"Whitney writes to me a lot," Lana said, handing

Clark another piece of tape. "He always asks how the Crows are doing. I wrote back that we had yet another new coach, which doesn't exactly lend itself to team spirit. He misses football a lot. He misses . . . well, everything."

"That video you made for him was killer," Clark told her, taping a flyer to the office door.

The week before, Lana had made a new videotape for Whitney. She'd taped all Whitney's old friends sending him greetings, and she'd included Clark in it. When the camera was on him, Clark had tried to be upbeat and friendly. But he'd felt weirdly disloyal, knowing that he and Whitney were in love with the same girl.

"So, he loved it, right?" Clark asked.

"Um . . . not exactly." Lana ran her thumbnail along the ragged edge of the tape roll, her eyes so downcast that all Clark could see was a curtain of glossy hair.

"Um?" Clark echoed. "How could he not like it?"

Clark had learned that Lana had added a personal section at the end of the tape. Evidently, it had been pretty intimate — Lana's telling Whitney how much she missed his kisses, being in his arms, et cetera, et cetera. Although Clark hadn't seen this part, one of his best friends had — Chloe Sullivan. And Chloe was only too eager to fill Clark in about it. Chloe had also told Clark that Lana wasn't going to trust the tape to the post office. Instead, she was going to send it overnight to Whitney's military base.

Lana looked up at Clark sheepishly, her eyes sad under knitted brows.

"Actually, Clark, I have a confession to make." She bit her lower lip. "I feel monumentally stupid telling you this."

"Telling me what?"

She hesitated. "Well, the truth is . . . I never sent it to Whitney."

Clark was floored. "Why not?"

"I wish I knew."

She leaned her back against the glass trophy case. "The thing is, I added all this personal stuff at the end, and . . ."

Clark mumbled something ambiguous. He didn't really want to tell her that Chloe had already relayed that information.

"Well, I thought about just erasing that part,

and then sending it," Lana went on, "but it didn't feel right. So I taped over it with something else, and I hated that, too. So I tried again. But it still wasn't any good. That's why it's still in an envelope at home."

Clark knew it was wrong, but happiness tap-danced across his skin. He could think of only one reason why Lana wouldn't want to send the personal messages of love she'd recorded to Whitney: She wasn't really sure if she loved him.

Which might mean that Lana and I —

Clark came crashing back to Earth as he recalled Whitney's last words to him before he got on the bus to leave for basic training: "Take care of Lana for me, Clark."

And Clark had agreed. Not wholeheartedly, but at the moment, right before the spring formal last year, he didn't see another way out.

What kind of person moves in on a girl after that?

"Well, I'm sure you know what you're doing, Lana," he said, careful not to meet her eyes.

"Actually, Clark, when it comes to my personal life, I don't know what I'm doing at all," Lana confessed. "I've given it a lot of thought. There's a reason that I couldn't commit to him before he left."

"What is it?" Clark asked.

This time her gaze was so direct that he couldn't escape it. "You know how they say the truth will set you free, Clark? Well, the truth is —"

"Yes?" he prompted.

She sighed and glanced away for a moment. "You know, sometimes it's hard for the person telling the truth to know if she's ready to tell the total truth. Like, did you ever tell anyone that you would do something, because you didn't want to hurt them in the moment, but the truth was that you weren't ready to do what they asked you to do at all?"

Clark swallowed hard.

More than you know, Lana.

Lana looped her hair behind her ears and offered him a crooked smile. "Sorry. I'm not usually so cryptic. Why don't I start putting up flyers in the other hallway? I've got another roll of tape." She pulled it from her pocket, took a pile of the flyers, and disappeared around the corner.

Clark scuffed a shoe against the linoleum in

frustration. What had Lana been trying to tell him? That her feelings for him were stronger than her feelings for Whitney?

What did she mean when she said, "The truth will set you free"?

He was lost in his own musings, but suddenly something made him go on full alert: the smell of smoke. Clark whipped around, gasping at what met his eyes. All the way down the hall, every single flyer they'd put up was now on the floor.

And all of them were on fire.

Chapter 2

"So the flyers caught fire, then they burned out, and that's the end of the story. Right, Clark?" Chloe asked Clark, as she pulled into a spot in the municipal lot downtown. "Frankly, it's barely worth a paragraph in the *Torch*. Now, if the sprinkler system had come on . . ."

Actually, I super-sped down the hallway and crushed out each fire with my bare hands before the sprinkler system even came on, Clark thought. *That's probably worth more than a paragraph. But I guess I'll leave out that part.*

It was the next evening, and Clark couldn't get the weird fires out of his mind. There had been no damage because he'd put the flames out so quickly. A fire engine did show up, but there was nothing for the firemen to do. Clark and Lana gave statements to the chief, but neither had any idea how the fires had started.

Now, Chloe and Clark headed down Main Street toward Smallville's town hall, where they were due for a meeting. "I'm surprised at you, Chloe," Clark said. "Aren't you the girl who has a woo-woo theory about everything weird that happens in this town?"

"A few little baby fires set by vandals is hardly Wall of Weird–worthy, Clark."

"I'm talking about twenty flyers we'd just put up," Clark emphasized. "All of them were on the floor, and all of them were on fire. Twenty separate fires burning simultaneously, Chloe. If that's not Wall of Weird material, then how do you explain it?"

The Wall of Weird was a bulletin board in the office of the school newspaper, the *Torch*. Chloe herself had put it together; on the Wall of Weird were newspaper and magazine clippings of all the strange and peculiar things that seemed to happen in Smallville.

Chloe shook her head. "Nope. This time, it's

just a bunch of jerks playing with your mind. Ten kids following you, pulling down the flyers, lighting them with matches."

"We were alone," Clark maintained. "And we closed the doors behind us."

"They came in through the window, then," Chloe said. She stood on tiptoe to kiss his cheek. "It's sweet that you're trying to find Wall of Weird material for me, Clark. *Asante*," she added, thanking him in Swahili.

"*Je! Iko namna*," Clark replied.

"Showoff. Care to translate?"

"Literally, 'Is there a way?' What it means, though, is: Something suspicious is going on."

Chloe rolled her eyes. "Honestly, Clark, you memorize things faster than is humanly possible. You could probably read *War and Peace* in Swahili by now. Or maybe you're fooling everyone and learning Russian, too."

"*Nyet*," Clark joked. "Only Swahili."

It's because my supermemory is developing right along with the rest of my superpowers, he thought. But of course, some things were best not discussed.

"You're the one who gets straight A's in French," he said instead.

Chloe checked her watch. "We'd better hustle. We're already late."

At least they were late for a good reason. He and Chloe had made a quick trip to the main library in Metropolis to do research for a paper they were writing together for American History class. Chloe's car had gotten a flat soon after they'd left the city. She'd insisted on helping him change the tire. With her standing by his side, he'd had to change the tire the old-fashioned way — minus his superpowers. Which meant it took thirty minutes to do what he could easily have done in thirty seconds.

"You ought to consider race walking in the Olympics, Clark." Chloe was taking three steps to every one of his just to keep up with him.

"I can carry you faster than you're jogging."

"I guess that means my odds of winning the next Metropolis marathon are between slim and none. And if we weren't here already, I'd take you up on your offer," Chloe quipped.

When they reached town hall, a bright red-on-white banner was stretched across the front, from one white pillar to the next, announcing the multicultural festival. They pushed through the double doors. "Wouldn't you think that a town large enough to hold a multicultural festival would have earned the right to call itself 'Mediumville'?" Chloe asked.

"I like Smallville named Smallville, thanks," Clark said as they reached the meeting room. The door was still open; both he and Chloe were happily surprised to find that the meeting hadn't yet been called to order.

"Yo, Clark! Chloe!" Pete Ross called out, waving to them. Pete was near the front of the room, sitting with Lana and their new friend, Shaaban Mwariri, who had recently moved to Smallville with his parents from Tanzania in East Africa, and another friend, Tina Wu. It was Shaaban, who was named for a famous Tanzanian poet, who'd been teaching them Swahili.

"We were wondering where you were," Tina said, scooching over so that Clark and Chloe could join them. "My grandmother has already come over three times to ask about you."

Clark looked across the room at the elderly Mrs. Wu, who caught his glance and smiled broadly at him, bobbing her head up and down. "Why would she do that?" Clark asked.

"Because she has a massive crush on you," Tina explained. "I'm completely serious. She says you are almost as nice as the boys she knew in Singapore. Trust me when I tell you that's her concept of a high compliment."

"I guess we'll have to start planning your dowry, Clark," Lana teased, and then she changed the subject. "I was just telling them about the fires. I still can't figure out how all those flyers ignited at the same time."

"Honestly?" Chloe began. "Compared to some of the truly bizarre stuff that goes on in this town, that was small potatoes."

"Yeah. Now if Ballister's American History classroom had burned down . . ." Pete began. He looked at the front of the room and scowled. Mr. Ballister was on the town council, and was seated behind a table on a small raised stage with the other bigwigs.

"You'd do anything to get out of his class," Tina said, laughing.

"The man hates me," Pete maintained. "It's personal. I'm serious."

"Why would he hate you?" Tina asked, looking utterly unconvinced.

Instead of answering, Pete posed another question. "How come he doesn't go to the church Clark and I go to? It's only a block from his house."

Shaaban scratched his chin. "I have no idea what you're driving at, man."

"Maybe our church is a little too interracial for him," Pete suggested. "That's why he's going to the church over in Jaspar. It's all white."

"Pete, I think you're making a mountain out of nothing. Ballister has taught American History at Smallville High forever," Lana pointed out. "He was my Aunt Nell's teacher. I doubt that a racist would be teaching American History."

"Not to mention the fact that he's on the multicultural festival committee," Clark added.

Pete sighed. "Forget it," he mumbled under his breath. He looked at Clark. "So, where were you guys?"

"We got a flat coming back from Metropolis," Chloe explained. "Wouldn't you think that the library here would have the right archival materials on Smallville history so that we wouldn't have to schlep to the city?"

Shaaban's dark eyes twinkled. "Who are you kidding, Chloe? You'd make any excuse to go to Metropolis," he teased, in his musical East African accent.

"Okay, so I'm not a small-town girl at heart," Chloe admitted.

"Neither am I," Lana said. "Once I graduate, it's on to college and out of here."

Clark nodded. He knew that Chloe had lived in Metropolis until just a few years earlier, when her dad had brought the family to Smallville so he could go to work at the Luthorcorp fertilizer factory. He understood how she might still long for the bright lights and the big city. But Lana was a different story. She'd lived in Smallville since she was a toddler.

Maybe she wants to get out of Smallville for a different reason.

Lana had been just three when she and her parents had come to Smallville from Metropolis for a day of fun. Little Lana had put on her favorite fairy princess outfit and stayed with her Aunt Nell so her parents could go to the annual Smallville High School homecoming game.

It was on that day, twelve years ago, that the spaceship carrying Clark had plummeted to Earth in a massive meteor shower. One of those crashing meteorites had killed Lana's parents before the little girl's horrified eyes.

Something like that scars you for life. How could you ever feel at home in a town you'd only been visiting, where such an awful thing happened to your parents? And how could you possibly not hate the guy responsible?

Clark shuddered. Whenever he daydreamed about confiding in Lana, he tried to avoid thinking about the part where he'd have to tell her that the death of her parents was — in a way — his fault.

Shaaban's lilt pulled Clark out of his musings.

"It just so happens that Smallville is a very progressive little community," he said, trying to keep a straight face. "For example, every dwelling has indoor plumbing."

Tina clunked him playfully on the head with her notebook. Shaaban and his parents hailed from the capital of Tanzania — a place called Dar es Salaam. Shaaban's father was a renowned expert in the agriculture of underdeveloped nations, and Lex Luthor had brought Dr. Mwariri to Smallville to help develop a master plan to expand Luthorcorp markets in that direction.

In the brief time he'd been in Smallville, Shaaban and Clark had become good friends; their two families had also gotten acquainted. Along with Pete Ross and his parents, they all attended the same nondenominational church. After having talked to Shaaban's dad, Jonathan Kent had confirmed for Clark that Dr. Mwariri was indeed an agricultural genius.

Dr. Mwariri was also a born storyteller, spinning the wildest tales of his travels around the world and into the heart of Africa. Dr. Mwariri grew up in a tiny mountain village, near the border with Kenya, that didn't have electricity or plumbing, hence Shaaban's plumbing joke. But Clark knew that at Shaaban's home in Dar es Salaam, they had the same modern conveniences that his friends had in America.

"What's holding up the meeting?" Chloe asked, peering around the room.

"You see a rich, bald guy in the vicinity?" Pete asked rhetorically, meaning that Lex Luthor hadn't yet arrived. Pete disliked Lex intensely — he was sure that Lex's dad had taken advantage of Pete's own father years before in a business deal.

Pete didn't try to hide his loathing for Lex. It was problematic for Clark, who often felt stuck in the middle, since Pete and Lex were his two best friends. Clark often tried to point out that it was unfair to blame Lex for the sins of his father, but Pete wasn't buying it.

"Personally, I think Lex Luthor is hot," Tina said, folding her arms.

"Last week you told me that you thought Justin Timberlake was hot," Chloe reminded her.

"We won't even mention the lame factor on that one."

"Don't worry, Tina, a case of boys on the brain isn't fatal," Lana assured her.

Tina shrugged. "According to my grandmother, I'm not allowed to date until I'm married," she joked. "And I'm only allowed to marry a boy from Singapore . . . though she might make an exception for you, Clark."

Clark chuckled. "I'm honored."

"Let me just go check that out with your grandmother," Chloe said, pretending to get up. Tina laughed and tugged her back down to her seat.

"Pete, I still don't understand your dislike for Mr. Luthor," Shaaban said. "He treats my family very well. And the multicultural festival was his notion, after all."

"Hey, if money can buy it, so can Lex," Pete said darkly. "Anyway, I should be home catching up on my homework. Whose idea was it for us to be on this committee, anyway?"

"Yours," Chloe reminded him. "We're getting extra credit for American History, remember?

Which kind of undercuts your theory about Ballister being a racist, come to think of it. I think the real problem is that right now, you've got a C in his class."

Shaaban clapped Pete on the back. "No need to frown. I guarantee that after this meeting, you're in for one of the best meals of your entire life."

Clark smiled. Shaaban's parents had invited them all over to their home after the meeting for a traditional Tanzanian feast.

"Bring it on," Pete said, brightening. "I can't wait to taste that . . . what'd you call it again — uglie?"

Shaaban laughed. "*Ugali*. Ooh-GAH-lee."

"Ugly," Pete joked, and they all laughed.

"So sorry all," Lex Luthor apologized as he strode into the room, immediately taking his place behind the long table on the stage. "I was unavoidably detained."

With Lex on the scene, the meeting quickly got down to business. Ms. Parson, a middle school teacher whom Lex had selected to cochair the event, gave her progress report. She'd been Clark's teacher in eighth grade, and the Parsons had been in Smallville for many generations. That her family had always been leaders of the community was one of the reasons Lex had selected her. She spoke quickly about the various activities that would take place at the community gathering set for Sunday in the high school gym. At the main event, there would be cultural presentations and food from all the countries and cultures represented in modern Smallville. She finished by looking directly at Clark and his friends.

"And now I'd like to call on our teen committee to report on their performance this Sunday," Ms. Parson said, nodding in the teens' direction.

Clark nudged Tina. "You're on."

Tina stood and cleared her throat. "The teen committee plans to offer performance art representing twelve different cultures," she reported. "There will be dance, music, drama, and poetry, all representing the cultural diversity of our high school."

There were appreciative nods around the room.

"Question, Ms. Wu," Mr. Ballister called out sharply. Everyone knew he had badly wanted Ms. Parson's job as head of the festival. But, though he was two decades Ms. Parson's senior, Lex had passed him by. Lex had told Clark that for the first multicultural festival, he wanted to have a woman in charge, because that also would send a message that times were changing. "Will members of these different cultures be performing solo?"

"I don't understand why it matters," Tina responded matter-of-factly.

Mr. Ballister tugged on the side of his silver moustache. "My point being, while it's very nice to expose our students and the community to these performances, the learning curve seems limited unless the maximum number of people participate."

"Yes," Tina agreed. "That's why we plan to have many other students involved, also. For example, all the teens on our committee have agreed to do an African dance performance with Shaaban. In native dress."

What? Clark thought. *When did that happen?*

He looked at his friends. Clearly, they were also taken by surprise.

"And we'll have groups involved in performances and demonstrations that represent cultures other than their own," Tina added emphatically.

Even Mr. Ballister couldn't find any fault with that idea. Ms. Parson lavished praise on Tina before turning the meeting over to Lex.

As soon as Tina sat down, Pete leaned close to her. "Since when are we doing African dance?" he hissed.

"So I got carried away," Tina whispered back loudly enough so that Clark could hear.

Mr. Ballister looked sternly in the kids' direction. They stopped whispering; Lex flashed Clark an enigmatic smile.

"As I was saying," Lex continued, "Smallville is the new face of America. Just as America is changing, so is Smallville . . . and with tremendous speed. We can embrace this as progress, or we can live in a narrow-minded little box. America has always opened her arms to those from different cultures. I'm proud to see Smallville embracing these sons and daughters, just as I like to think that you've embraced me as one of your own."

Pete stifled an incredulous guffaw and poked Clark in the ribs. Lex finished up by thanking everyone for working so hard on the festival, and then passing out some T-shirts he'd had made. Clark couldn't help noticing that Pete was the only person in the room who didn't take one.

CHAPTER 3

Shaaban's house was within easy walking distance from downtown, so everyone left their cars where they had parked them and strolled the few blocks to the Mwariris' house.

"You guys, we all have to do the dance with Shaaban," Tina pleaded, "or I'll look like a liar."

"If the shoe fits," Pete pointed out.

"I wasn't lying, I was anticipating," Tina corrected him. She put her palms together as if she were praying. "Please-please-please-please."

"I think it'll be fun," Lana said.

"Bless you," Tina cried, grabbing Lana's arm.

"Yeah, I'm in," Chloe agreed, albeit reluctantly.

"Guys?" Tina turned to Pete and Clark.

Pete shook his head. "I am not getting on stage in some strange costume and dancing around in front of the entire town."

"But you're African American," Shaaban pointed out.

"Well, of course," Pete replied proudly. "And my family has been in Smallville as long as anyone's. I'm down with the Africa thing, too. But the dance is out. I'm sure my man Clark feels the same way I do."

Tina gave Clark a puppy-dog look. "Clark?"

What flew into Clark's mind was the time he'd been cast as Cyrano de Bergerac in the school play. He'd never in a million years thought he could do it, yet he'd managed to overcome his stage fright.

Not that I actually got to play the part, he recalled. *I had to fight off an invisible girl bent on destroying the theater. Why is it that fighting evil always seems to interfere with the rest of my life?*

"Clark-ie," Tina sang. "You're not going to fail me, are you?"

"Clarkie's sticking with me," Pete insisted.

"I don't know . . ." Clark wavered. Acting was one thing; African dance in "native dress" was another.

"Oh, come on," Shaaban said, nudging Clark's elbow. "What are you afraid of, man?"

"Looking like an idiot in front of the entire town comes to mind," Clark said.

Shaaban nodded. "Okay, here's my offer. After dinner, my father and I will show you the dance I have in mind. You'll see how cool it is. All the modern hip-hop moves have been borrowed from African dance."

"Yeah, but they don't wear grass skirts while they do it," Pete insisted.

"Grass skirts are Hawaiian, Pete," Lana said.

"Whatever. You get my point."

The group turned up the walkway to Shaaban's home; Shaaban led them around on the driveway to a side door. "My mom's car isn't here," he noted as he let them into the kitchen. "She must not be back from shopping for our feast yet. Come on in and I'll put on some music from home. You can hear what —"

Shaaban stopped in mid-sentence, too shocked to speak.

They were standing in his family's kitchen. It looked as if something had exploded in the room. There was broken glass and cutlery everywhere. The refrigerator door dangled open, food littered the floor. Every chair was overturned or broken. The beautiful carved wooden table was flooded with fresh red paint that still dripped to the floor.

"Dear God," Shaaban whispered hoarsely.

"Someone call the police," Clark said. Then, moving so fast that the world around him stopped dead, Clark super-sped through the house, looking for an intruder. He always thought of speeding along like this as going into "Clark time," because while he was fine, everything around him seemed frozen.

His last stop was the living room. It, too, was a disaster area. But what he found in there turned his stomach more than all the other damage put together.

He sped back to his friends and stepped out of

Clark time. "Let's check the living room," he said quietly.

Shaaban was the first one into the living room. There were tears in his eyes as he read what was spray-painted on the wall:

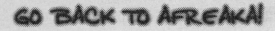

GO BACK TO AFREAKA!

CHAPTER 4

Clark whirled when he heard someone come through the open side door of the Mwariri house. It was too soon for the police to be there, yet. Was it the nutcase who had done this returning to the scene of the crime?

No. It wasn't the vandal. It was Shaaban's father.

"Dad?" Shaaban asked, his voice small.

Clark watched Dr. Mwariri's jaw fall open as he took in the ruins that was now his kitchen.

"Someone must have broken in, sir," Clark told him.

"I already called the police," Lana added.

Dr. Mwariri's hand went over his mouth, as if to say that the horror of this was unspeakable.

"How could this have happened?" he finally asked. "It isn't possible. This is *America*."

"We don't have much crime here in Smallville," Pete assured him, not wanting him to think badly of the entire town.

"Is the rest of the house —?"

"Trashed," his son filled in bleakly. "I'm afraid so. And in the living room . . ."

Clark could see that Shaaban couldn't bring himself to tell his dad what had been painted on their living room wall.

"This is not possible," Dr. Mwariri insisted.

Before he could explain what he meant, the wailing siren of a police cruiser that had pulled into the driveway interrupted him. Clark recognized Deputy Sheriff Wayne Melrose when he got out. Melrose was in his fifties, a flinty-eyed man with a steel gray crew cut. His son, Mark, was in his class. Way back in grade school, Mark had proudly introduced his dad to the kids at an all-school assembly. Clark remembered how Deputy Melrose used Mark to demonstrate what to do if a stranger tried to talk to them, or tried to pull them into a car. Even then, Clark had thought there was just something *hard* about the guy.

Clark, Pete, Lana, and Chloe waited in the kitchen while Shaaban and his dad took Sheriff Melrose on a tour of their wrecked home. They were all so shocked and depressed about what had happened that they barely spoke.

A hate crime in Smallville. Clark couldn't wrap his mind around it. *Not here. In Metropolis, maybe, but not here. I should call my parents. They'll want to know.*

Rather than use the family phone, in case the sheriff planned to dust it for fingerprints, Clark borrowed Lana's cell and called his parents. He spoke to his dad, who was stunned by the news and said he and Martha would be right over.

Deputy Melrose took pictures of everything and then assembled everyone on the back patio to take their statements. He started with Dr. Mwariri. "Now, if you could explain it to me again, sir," Deputy Melrose said, taking out his pad and pen.

"It is as I said," Dr. Mwariri insisted. "I was home the whole time."

"You were what?" Clark blurted out.

"I was *here*, I tell you."

"But you came in from outside!" Clark continued.

"You're Clark Kent, correct?" Deputy Melrose asked sharply.

"Yes, sir."

"Son, when I want to hear from you, I'll ask you."

"Sorry," Clark said, bursting with frustration.

"It's not so complicated. I was outside for only a minute!" Dr. Mwariri exclaimed. "I have a garden in the backyard, and I was adding some organic material to the compost pile."

The sheriff looked skeptical. "Maybe you were out there longer than you thought, sir."

Dr. Mwariri was emphatic. "I am telling you, I know how long I was outside. I went outside right after I finished watching the news. The five o'clock news," he added emphatically. "It ended at six."

"We got here at five after six," Tina put in. "I

remember looking at my watch because I promised my grandmother I'd check in with her at six-thirty."

"Your watch may have been slow, or it could have stopped," the sheriff suggested.

A thought struck Clark. "I think I can prove we arrived at five after six." He stood. "I'll be right back."

"Kent, get back here!" the sheriff called after him.

But Clark jogged into the kitchen just ahead of a group of crime investigators who were about to search the place. He remembered something he'd seen with his X-ray vision when they came in the kitchen — a small clock on the floor that had slid into a space between the fridge and a counter. Making sure no one was in sight, he hoisted the refrigerator with one hand, grabbed the clock with a nearby paper towel, and righted the refrigerator again.

Bingo, Clark thought, looking at the clock. He hustled back to Melrose and his friends, and handed the clock to the sheriff.

"I found it on the kitchen floor," Clark quickly explained. "The battery fell out. It was probably on the kitchen counter before the rampage, and the battery fell out when the culprit knocked it off. Look at the time."

The clock time read 6:05 P.M.

"So that's what time the attack must have taken place," Chloe concluded.

But that isn't possible, Clark thought. *It just isn't possible.*

"Tina was right," Lana said, reading the clock.

"What do you kids think this is, a *Nancy Drew* book?" Melrose barked.

"Sir, Clark just handed you proof of the time of the attack!" Pete exclaimed.

"This is conclusive of nothing," Deputy Melrose said, narrowing his eyes at Clark. "Do you realize you just compromised a crime scene? You moved evidence and your fingerprints are now on the clock."

Clark reddened. "No. That's why I used a paper towel. I thought —"

"Do me a favor, don't think," the sheriff said sharply. He dropped the clock into an evidence bag. "Maybe the hands of the clock were moved when the perp knocked it over. Or maybe you moved them, Kent."

"This doesn't make any sense!" Dr. Mwariri was growing more and more frustrated with the sheriff. "Our home was fine when I went out back. Fine! If someone had come in and done this much damage when I was outside, don't you think I would have heard him? Or them? But the clock says that's when it happened."

"With all due respect, sir, I don't answer the questions. I just ask them," Deputy Melrose said, his voice icy. "Let's go over this again. You were watching the news —"

"Donneth? Are you all right?" Jonathan Kent asked as he and Martha hurried around the house to the patio.

Dr. Mwariri stood up and gratefully embraced his friends. "It was so good of you to come."

"Clark called us," Martha explained. "Where's Sarah?"

"Thank God she hadn't arrived home yet," Dr. Mwariri replied. "I'm fine, and so is Shaaban."

"Physically, anyway," Shaaban muttered.

Deputy Melrose stood up. "Jonathan. Martha."

"Wayne," Jonathan said curtly. Clark could tell by the way that his father said "Wayne" that Jonathan didn't care much for the deputy sheriff.

"The last thing we need is more people at this crime scene," muttered Melrose.

"We won't go in the house while your detectives are gathering evidence. But we don't intend to leave, either," Martha said. "The Mwariris are our friends."

"Figures," the sheriff muttered so low he could barely be heard.

"What did you just say?" Jonathan demanded.

Deputy Melrose's gaze met his. "I said it figures. What I meant was, it figures a stand-up guy like you would stand by his friends."

Clark wasn't convinced that that's what the sheriff had meant at all, but he didn't say anything. His dad didn't look too convinced, either.

"One hate crime in Smallville is one too many," Jonathan insisted. "We have to get this guy."

"*Apparent* hate crime," Deputy Melrose corrected. "Frankly, I don't know what we have here."

That was more than Clark could take. "Hold on, sir. You're not accusing Dr. Mwariri of wrecking his own house, are you?"

"That's ludicrous," Martha said, agreeing with her son.

"I'm not accusing anyone of anything. Yet," the deputy pointedly added.

Shaaban's eyes went stormy, his voice tight. "My father is an honorable man."

"I second that," Jonathan said. "Your theory is absurd and insulting."

"Exactly," Pete emphatically agreed. "Besides, why would anyone trash his own house and leave racist graffiti on the wall?"

Deputy Melrose ticked the possible reasons off his fingers. "Attention. Sympathy. Publicity. To frame someone. I could go on."

"Are you out of your mind?" Clark asked. His father put a restraining hand on his arm. "I'm sorry, Dad, but we can't just stand here and let him make these accusations!"

"I have no theory and I've made no accusations," the deputy reminded them. "I do know, doctor, that the facts as you've reported them are a physical impossibility."

"The 'facts' go like this," Lana began deliberately. "This is a hate crime. The people who did this are trying to drive a family out of Smallville. Who knows what they'll do next?"

"*Mchzea wembe humkata mwenyewe,*" Shaaban muttered darkly.

"He who plays with a razor, cuts himself," Clark translated.

Shaaban nodded. "In other words, if you play with fire, you get burned."

"You're right, Shaaban," Clark agreed. "Whoever did this is not going to get away with it. I promise you that."

CHAPTER 5

"He's not my favorite person in Smallville," Jonathan admitted as he and Clark watched Deputy Melrose pull away from the house in his cruiser. "But he's always been a good sheriff."

"Maybe you don't know him as well as you think you know him, Dad," Clark said.

Before Dr. Mwariri went out front to wait for his wife (he wanted to prepare her, rather than have her walk in on the horrible scene), he insisted that other than the Kents, the rest of Shaaban's friends go to their respective homes. Not that he didn't appreciate their support, but he wanted to restore his home to relative calm as quickly as possible. Lana, Chloe, Pete, and Tina did depart, but not before promising they'd help out in any way they could, and reminding Shaaban that they were only a phone call away.

When Sarah Mwariri returned, she walked wordlessly past the Kents, and into the house with her husband. When they emerged together, a few minutes later, she was badly shaken.

"No one is hurt," she said, hugging her son. "That's the most important thing."

"This is not what Smallville is about," Jonathan Kent said, for probably the sixth time.

"It's all right, Jonathan," Sarah said. "We don't hold the town responsible for the actions of one sick person."

"Why don't you come and stay with us?" Martha asked her.

Sarah and her husband exchanged a glance. "Thank you, but I think we'll stay right here," Dr. Mwariri said.

"I don't think that's a very good idea," Jonathan said. "It's still a mess, and a crime scene. This could just be some stupid prank, but it could also be a lot more serious."

"Please come stay at the farm with us?" Martha asked again.

Sarah hesitated. "I don't know . . ."

"There's plenty of room," Clark encouraged. "Shaaban and I could sleep in the loft, and you and Dr. Mwariri could take my room."

I only wish I could explain that our farm is the safest place they could possibly be, Clark thought.

Dr. Mwariri shook his head. "We appreciate the generosity of your offer. But no one is going to run us out of our own —"

"Donneth? Sarah?" Lex Luthor strode up the driveway, his face ashen. "I came as soon as I heard the news. Are you all right?"

"We're all okay, Mr. Luthor," Shaaban assured him.

Clark wasn't surprised that Lex had learned about the crime. Smallville was aptly named; news traveled fast.

"I want you to know that Luthorcorp stands by its employees," Lex said. "I'll do whatever it takes to catch the people who did this to you — and to protect your home and property."

"Funny, Lex. I never thought of you as a white knight," Jonathan said dryly.

Clark shook his head. His dad was like Pete in

the way his long-standing animosity toward Lionel Luthor spilled over to Lex; nothing Clark said or did seemed to sway his opinion.

"I assure you, Jonathan," Lex began, "when it comes to friends and members of the Luthorcorp family of employees, I will charge into hell to vanquish any foe." He turned to the Mwariris. "I can offer you a great deal more protection under my roof at the mansion. I hope you'll be my house guests until this crime is solved."

"We've already invited them to stay at the farm," Jonathan told Lex.

"Nonsense," Lex insisted. "They'll stay with me. We have state-of-the-art security." He turned back to the Mwariris. "You and your son will have the entire north guest wing to yourselves. You'll be more than comfortable, I can assure you. The mansion is the absolute safest place you can be."

Trust me, Clark thought. *That's not true.*

Sarah took her husband's hand. "Donneth, I think we should accept the Kents' kind offer. It's prudent. Shaaban will be with his friend. It's only for a little while. We will be back as soon as the police say we can."

Her husband nodded reluctantly.

"Son?" She waited for Shaaban's reply.

He nodded, and added to Clark, "Thanks, man."

Mrs. Mwariri turned to Lex. "We appreciate your generous offer. Nonetheless, I think we're going to accept the Kents' invitation. We know them personally, after all."

If Lex felt at all slighted by Dr. Mwariri's decision, he didn't show it. "That's fine, Donneth," he said. "You won't mind if I arrange for a private security service to keep an eye on your home while you're with the Kents?"

"Thank you, but it's not necessary," Dr. Mwariri replied.

"I think it's a good idea, sir," Clark said.

"I do, too, Dad," Shaaban said.

"It's settled, then," Lex said. "I feel somewhat responsible for this, Dr. Mwariri. It was my job offer that brought you to Smallville. Nothing would give me more pleasure than to catch the idiot who did this to you."

Me neither, Clark thought, *and I'm just the guy to do it. The first thing I'm going to do is to find out where Deputy Melrose was while the Mwariris' house was being trashed. Because sometimes, the answer is right under your own nose.*

CHAPTER 6

GENESIS JOURNAL, ENTRY #1

OH, MAN. I AM INVINCIBLE. I AM SUPER.
I CAN RULE THE WORLD.

IT WORKED TO PERFECTION. THIS RUSH
CAME OVER ME WHILE I WAS TRASHING THE
AFRICANS' HOUSE. IT WAS EVEN BETTER
THAN SETTING THE FIRES AT SCHOOL.
NOW I KNOW, I CAN DO ANYTHING.
EVERYTHING. NO ONE CAN STOP ME.

I FULLY REALIZE THAT SOMEDAY THIS
JOURNAL WILL BE A HISTORICAL DOCUMENT
OF MOMENTOUS PROPORTIONS. MY NAME
WILL BE FAMOUS. MY STORY WILL BE
STUDIED IN TEXTBOOKS AND AT THE
GREAT SCIENCE LABS OF THE WORLD. THIS
IS WHY I'M GOING TO RECORD IT ALL HERE,
SO THAT THE WORLD WILL UNDERSTAND.

LET HISTORY RECORD THAT THE FIRST
DAY OF GENESIS WAS TWO DAYS AGO,
WEDNESDAY. SHE WOKE ME UP WITH THE
USUAL DRONE: WHY IS YOUR ROOM SUCH A
MESS? ALL YOU DO IS STAY IN YOUR ROOM
AND WORK ON YOUR COMPUTER. YOU USED
TO DO ART AND SING IN THE CHURCH CHOIR
AND HAVE NICE FRIENDS. WHAT IS WRONG
WITH YOU?

SHE'S SO BANAL. SO UTTERLY
PREDICTABLE.

I'M LIKE: THERE'S NO SCHOOL, IT'S AN
IN-SERVICE DAY FOR TEACHERS, I WANT
TO SLEEP. I'M SURE THE WORDS CAME
OUT OF MY MOUTH BUT EVER SINCE <u>HE</u>
CAME INTO MY LIFE SHE DOESN'T HEAR
ANYTHING I SAY. SO SHE HAULED ME OUT
OF BED AND THE RANT WENT SOMETHING
LIKE: CLEAN UP YOUR ROOM TAKE A
SHOWER DO YOUR CHORES DO YOUR HOME-
WORK YOU'RE SO SMART WHY DO YOU GET
BAD GRADES YOU'RE SO LAZY YOU USED
TO BE A GOOD KID WHAT HAPPENED TO
YOU AND ON AND ON AND ON AND ON UN-
TIL I COULDN'T THINK OR EVEN
BREATHE BECAUSE SHE WAS <u>SUCKING ALL
THE AIR RIGHT OUT OF THE ROOM.</u>

SHE REFERRED TO <u>HIM</u> AS "YOUR DAD" AGAIN. I'VE ONLY TOLD HER TEN ZILLION TIMES THAT I HATE HIS GUTS AND <u>HE'S</u> NOT GOING TO BE MY DAD EVEN IF SHE DECIDES TO MARRY HIM LIKE SHE SAYS SHE WILL. I SAID TO HER FACE: "I'VE GOT A REAL DAD, REMEMBER?" IT'S LIKE SHE DOESN'T EVEN HEAR ME. I COULD FEEL THE REDS COMING ON, WHICH IS WHAT I CALL THE FEELING THAT COMES OVER ME WHEN I GET REALLY MAD. NO — BEYOND MAD, TO A PLACE WHERE THERE IS NOTHING BUT GLOWING, PULSATING CRIMSON, AND I FEEL LIKE A HUMAN TIME BOMB WAITING TO EXPLODE.

I TRIED TO CONCENTRATE ON SOMETHING OTHER THAN THE SOUND OF HER WHINE, AND MY EYES FELL ON THE PRESENT MY REAL DAD MADE FOR ME. THE DAY BEFORE, TUESDAY, I HAD FOUND THE PACKAGE ON MY BED. INSIDE WAS THIS AWESOME HOURGLASS. IT'S REALLY AMAZING-LOOKING, FULL OF GLOWING WHITE SAND WITH GREEN FLECKS. HERE IS WHAT THE CARD SAID:

SON, I HOPE THIS WILL REMIND YOU OF THE GOOD OLD DAYS. EVERY TIME YOU

LOOK AT IT, YOU'LL KNOW THAT I
WISH WE COULD GO BACK TO A TIME
WHEN WE WERE STILL TOGETHER, AND
JUST STOP IT RIGHT THERE.
LOVE, DAD.

LOOKING PAST HER AT MY HOURGLASS
MADE THE REDS MORE BEARABLE. I KNEW
IF I WENT DOWN FOR BREAKFAST, SHE'D
START IN ON ME AGAIN. SO I HAD TO
GET OUT OF THERE. I THREW ON SOME
CLOTHES. RIGHT BEFORE I LEFT MY ROOM,
I TURNED THE HOURGLASS OVER FOR
THE VERY FIRST TIME. THEN I HEADED
FOR THE GARAGE TO GET MY OLD BIKE,
BECAUSE IT'S THE ONLY FORM OF TRANS-
PORTATION I'VE GOT WITHOUT GOING
TO <u>THEM</u> TO BORROW THE CAR. I DON'T
GO TO <u>THEM</u> FOR ANYTHING IF I CAN HELP
IT. I FIGURED I'D RIDE OUT INTO THE
COUNTRY AND JUST CHILL.
   MY ROUTE TOOK ME PAST THE TOWN
HALL AND A BIG SIGN FOR THEIR MULTI-
CULTURAL FESTIVAL. MY KNUCKLES WENT
WHITE ON THE HANDLEBARS. ONCE I GOT
OUT OF TOWN, I ZOOMED PAST A BUS

STOP ON THE OLD COUNTRY ROAD HARDLY ANYONE EVER TAKES ANYMORE, SINCE IT PARALLELS THE HIGHWAY. THERE'S STILL A BUS STOP OUT THERE, THOUGH. THIS OLD BLACK WOMAN AND A LITTLE GIRL WERE WAITING FOR THE BUS.

JEEZ. THEY WERE EVERYWHERE.

I WHIZZED PAST THE KENT FARM. I CAN'T STAND THAT CLARK KENT KID. HIS BEST FRIEND IS BLACK, THEY'RE ALL BUDDY-BUDDY WITH THE NEW KID FROM AFRICA — I CALL IT <u>AFREAKA</u> — AND THEY ALL GO TO THE CHURCH WHERE ALL THE RACES MIX. KENT'S ALWAYS STARING AT LANA LANG. I TRIED TO BE NICE TO LANA IN GRADE SCHOOL; SHE COULDN'T EVEN REMEMBER MY NAME. NO ONE CAN TELL ME THAT GIRL HAS PURE BLOOD IN HER, BUT EVERYONE AT SMALLVILLE HIGH THINKS SHE'S SO BEAUTIFUL. WHAT A JOKE.

WITH EVERY PUSH ON MY PEDALS I GOT MADDER, UNTIL I FELT A BAD CASE OF THE REDS COMING ON AGAIN. MY HEAD WAS POUNDING AND MY HEART FELT LIKE IT WOULD BURST OUT OF MY CHEST. I PEDALED FASTER AND FASTER, BUT YOU

CAN'T OUTRIDE THE REDS, AND SUD-
DENLY I BUMPED OVER SOMETHING — A
DRAINAGE PIPE STICKING OUT OF THE
PAVEMENT, I THINK. IT SENT ME OUT
OF CONTROL, CAREENING TOWARD THIS
FIELD WHERE SOME COWS WERE GRAZING.
THE NEXT THING I KNEW I WAS
FLYING OFF OF MY BIKE AND TUMBLING
THROUGH THE AIR, HEAD OVER FEET. I
LANDED IN THIS PILE OF HAY, THE WIND
KNOCKED OUT OF ME.

So I JUST LAY THERE FOR A MINUTE,
CATCHING MY BREATH AND MAKING SURE I
WAS ALL IN ONE PIECE. I DIDN'T REALIZE
ANYTHING WAS WEIRD UNTIL I SAT UP
AND LOOKED OVER AT THE COWS GRAZING
UNDER THIS ANCIENT, GNARLED TREE.

<u>THEY WEREN'T MOVING.</u>

OKAY. COWS DON'T ALWAYS MOVE ALL
THAT MUCH, BUT THIS WAS DIFFERENT;
THEY WERE ABSOLUTELY STILL. I LOOKED
UP. OVERHEAD THERE WAS A SOARING EAGLE.
HER SPREAD WINGS SEEMED PIERCED TO
THE BLUE SKY, AS IF SHE'D BEEN STUCK
THERE WITH PUSHPINS. I STARED AT
HER FOR A LONG TIME. AND THEN IT

DAWNED ON ME — THE CLOUDS BEHIND THE BIRD WEREN'T MOVING EITHER.

I LOOKED AROUND. THE LEAVES ON THE TREES WEREN'T DANCING IN THE BREEZE AND THE ALFALFA ON THE GROUND WASN'T RIPPLING IN THE WIND. IN FACT, THERE WAS NO WIND. BUT THIS IS KANSAS. THERE'S <u>ALWAYS</u> WIND.

THERE WAS ONLY ONE THING MOVING. ME.

I FIGURED I WAS IN SOME KIND OF NIGHTMARE, SO I PINCHED MYSELF. IT HURT. BUT I NEEDED ONE MORE TEST TO BE SURE THAT I WASN'T DREAMING.

I PICKED UP MY BIKE AND PEDALED BACK THE WAY I'D COME, PAST THE KENT FARM, TO THE BUS STOP. I FIGURED SINCE THE BUS HADN'T PASSED ME, THE OLD BLACK LADY AND THE LITTLE GIRL STILL HAD TO BE THERE, AND THEY WERE.

ONLY THEY WERE STATUES.

I DON'T KNOW WHAT MADE ME NOTICE THE GIRL'S WATCH. IT WAS ONE OF THOSE KIDDY THINGS WITH A PINK PLASTIC BAND AND FLOWERS ON IT. MAYBE IT WAS BECAUSE THE CHEAP LITTLE RHINESTONES

ON THE NUMBERS CAUGHT THE LIGHT.
ANYWAY, I WENT OVER TO THE BENCH
AND LOOKED AT IT. IT SAID THE TIME
WAS 8:30 A.M.

ONLY IT COULDN'T BE 8:30. I'D LEFT
MY HOUSE AT 8:15, BIKED MAYBE TWO
MILES BEFORE I GOT THROWN INTO THE
HAYSTACK. THEN I BIKED BACK A COUPLE
OF MILES TO THE BUS STOP, AND I'D
BEEN THERE A PRETTY LONG TIME. WHICH
MEANT IT HAD TO BE MORE LIKE NINE. SO
I CHECKED THE OLD LADY'S WATCH. IT
READ 8:30, TOO. I CRACKED UP IN SPITE
OF MYSELF. IT LOOKED LIKE THEY COULD
BE WAITING FOR A REALLY, REALLY LONG
TIME, AT THIS RATE.

THEN I CHECKED MY OWN WATCH. 8:30
A.M. <u>AND THE SECOND HAND WASN'T MOV-
ING.</u>

I WENT OVER EVERYTHING THAT HAD
HAPPENED IN MY MIND, SAW MYSELF
HURTLING THROUGH SPACE WHEN I'D
BEEN THROWN FROM MY BIKE. AND THAT'S
WHEN IT CAME TO ME IN A FLASH OF PURE
BRILLIANCE.

<u>WHAT IF I HAD SOMEHOW PIERCED THE
FABRIC OF TIME?</u> WHAT IF I WAS MOVING

so fast that, in comparison, everything else seemed like it wasn't moving at all?

I pedaled back into town. Main Street was like a wax museum. Nothing moved. Nothing seemed real. Everything was frozen, except me.

I walked into the convenience store and took a candy bar. The cashier was frozen in the middle of handing change to some fat guy. I ate the candy right in front of her. She could have been dead for all the reaction I got.

Well, I knew what that meant. I could take the money out of her hand and no one would ever know. I could take all the money in the cash register, too. I could do anything.

Here's the part where you'll start to know the kind of person I really am. My dad raised me right. I am not a thief, not even when I am sure that I could get away with it. I didn't take a penny. Still, knowing I had the power to do anything I wanted was an amazing feeling.

But . . . if I stayed in fast time, I'd be alone. What if I couldn't get back to real time at all? That scared the pants off me but I forced myself to concentrate. I've read all this stuff on the Internet about wormholes in the space/time continuum. Maybe I'd torn a hole in it, somehow. Or maybe one had opened up for me. Lots of weird stuff has happened in Smallville, I thought. I remembered when the old football coach started fires with his mind, and when another kid started throwing cars around like they were toys. So why shouldn't one of those weird things happen to me?

The question was, how could I reverse the process? I read someplace that for every action, there is an equal and opposite reaction. So I rode back down the country road, past the frozen old lady and the little girl, past the Kent farm. I pedaled like a bat out of hell until I bumped the drainage pipe and

FELT MYSELF FALLING, FALLING, FALLING ALL OVER AGAIN.

THIS TIME I LANDED UNDER AN OLD TREE, LOOKING STRAIGHT UP INTO THIS COW'S DUMB ROUND EYES. SHE MOOED HER SURPRISE AT SEEING ME, AND BACKED AWAY.

HOLY MOLEY. IT WORKED.

THE WORLD WAS BACK TO NORMAL. THAT'S WHAT OTHER PEOPLE WOULD THINK, ANYWAY. BUT NOW THAT I HAD MADE THE GREATEST DISCOVERY OF ALL TIME, IT WOULD NEVER BE "NORMAL" FOR ME AGAIN.

ONE DAY, THIS JOURNAL WILL BE WORTH MILLIONS OF DOLLARS. I'LL BE KNOWN AS THE GUY WHO CONQUERED TIME. I COULD USE MY POWERS TO GET RICH IF I WANTED TO. HELL, I COULD ROB THE WHITE HOUSE AND NO ONE WOULD EVER KNOW IT WAS ME.

YESTERDAY, GENESIS DAY TWO, I FIGURED OUT HOW TO CONTROL THE POWER. AT FIRST, I ACTED LIKE AN IDIOT, RIDING MY BICYCLE AND BUMPING OVER THE DRAINAGE DITCH, AND FLYING THROUGH THE AIR. EVERY TIME I DID IT, WHEN I CAME

UP, THE WORLD WAS NORMAL. IT TOOK ME A DOZEN TIMES TO UNDERSTAND THAT I WASN'T GETTING THE POWER FROM THE DRAINAGE DITCH. IT HAD TO BE SOMETHING ELSE.

I FIGURED IT OUT BY ACCIDENT, WHEN I WENT BACK HOME AND TURNED OVER MY HOURGLASS, WATCHING THE GLOWING GREEN-FLECKED SAND SLIP THROUGH THE MINUTE OPENING AT ITS CENTER. JUST FOR FUN, I TOOK A LEAP ACROSS THE ROOM, ONTO MY BED.

AND I WAS IN THE ZONE.

I KNOW NOW THAT THE HOURGLASS IS THE CATALYST AND MY ABILITY TO AC-CELERATE TO WARP SPEED CAN BE ACCOM-PLISHED ANYWHERE, SO LONG AS I TURN OVER THE HOURGLASS AND THE SAND IS FLOWING. I'VE TIMED IT — THE HOURGLASS IS ACTUALLY A TWO-HOUR GLASS. ALL I HAVE TO DO IS FLIP IT OVER AND TAKE A RUNNING LEAP. SUDDENLY, I'M IN THE ZONE, THE FABRIC OF TIME TORN OPEN FOR ME. AND TO GET BACK TO NORMAL SPEED, I JUST HAVE TO WAIT FOR THE SAND TO GO THROUGH THE HOURGLASS. EVEN

WHEN I'M IN THE ZONE, SOMEHOW IT
JUST KEEPS GOING THROUGH THAT
HOURGLASS.

So, IT CAME TIME TO PUT THE ZONE
TO GOOD USE.

I BEGAN MY QUEST AND FOLLOWED
KENT AND STUCK-UP MISS LANG WHEN
THEY WENT INTO THE HIGH SCHOOL TO
PUT UP FLYERS FOR MULTICULTURAL
DAY. I BROUGHT THE HOURGLASS WITH
ME, AND FLIPPED IT OVER. I TOOK A BIG
RUNNING JUMP, AND BOOM! I WENT
RIGHT THROUGH THE TIME HOLE. IT WAS
SO EASY TO RIP THOSE STUPID FLYERS
DOWN AND SET THEM ON FIRE, AND SCARE
THE HELL OUT OF THEM. I DIDN'T
STICK AROUND, THOUGH, TO SEE WHAT
HAPPENED. WHEN THE SAND WAS THROUGH
THE HOURGLASS, I CAME BACK TO THE
WORLD.

TODAY, GENESIS DAY THREE, I WAS
READY TO MOVE ON TO BIGGER AND BET-
TER THINGS. I NEEDED A PLAN, AND MY
PLAN WAS THIS: I WOULD DRIVE THE
OTHERS OUT OF SMALLVILLE, AND IT
WOULD BE LIKE MY DAD SAID IT USED TO

BE. WHO BETTER TO START WITH THAN
THE AFRICANS? EVERY TIME I PASS
THAT KID SHAABAN IN THE HALL AT
SCHOOL, I WANT TO YELL INTO HIS FACE
THAT HE DOESN'T BELONG IN SMALLVILLE.
SHAABAN'S DAD HAS A GREAT JOB AT
LUTHORCORP, WHICH IS ONE LESS JOB IN
SMALLVILLE FOR A <u>REAL</u> AMERICAN.

So, EARLIER TONIGHT, I WENT INTO
THE ZONE AND WENT TO THE AFRICANS'
HOUSE. IT'S EVEN NICER THAN THE ONE
WE LIVED IN WHEN I WAS LITTLE, WHEN
WE WERE STILL A FAMILY. THAT GOT ME
MAD. HIS DAD WAS IN THE GARDEN, FROZEN,
BENT HALFWAY TO HIS PLANTS, SPREADING
SOME KIND OF COMPOST CRAP. I JUST
MARCHED ON INTO HIS HOUSE LIKE I WAS
KING OF THE CASTLE.

I TOOK MY TIME. GOT SOME LEMONADE
FROM THE REFRIGERATOR. TOOK A COUPLE
OF COOKIES. AND THEN I TRASHED THE
PLACE. NO ROCK STAR EVER TRASHED A HO-
TEL ROOM AS BAD AS I TRASHED THEIR
HOUSE. WHAT A RUSH. MY FINISHING TOUCH
WAS THE SPRAY PAINT SIGN I LEFT ON
THEIR LIVING ROOM WALL: GO BACK TO
AFREAKA!

FRIENDS, REAL AMERICANS, COUNTRYMEN,
LEND ME YOUR EARS. I COME TO BURY
THE OTHERS. IF THEY WANT PRAISE,
LET 'EM GO BACK WHERE THEY BELONG.
NOT IN MY TOWN. NOT IN SMALLVILLE.
    I'M GOING TO MAKE YOU SO PROUD OF
ME, DAD.

CHAPTER 7

At school on Monday, everyone was talking about the Friday attack on Shaaban's house. Clark was glad when he saw people come up to Shaaban in the hallways to tell him how horrible they thought it was. Over and over, his friend was assured that whoever did it was in no way representative of Smallville.

Principal Reynolds called an emergency assembly in the afternoon. As head of the upcoming festival, Ms. Parson gave a short speech; so did a wide variety of Smallville's religious leaders. They all talked about Smallville's tradition of tolerance and condemned the hate crime. Ms. Parson emphasized what a disgrace it was that this special week had been marred by this kind of incident.

Lex had also been invited to speak. In fact, he was delivering the closing address. "It is not enough that we stand together as citizens against this kind of hatred," Lex was saying now, his voice blazing. "We must unveil the truth, and find out who did this. We must seek speedy justice in order for all of us to believe that no one will get away with acts like this. Truth and justice — it's not just the American way. It's the Smallville way . . ."

There were murmurs and nods all around the auditorium. Next to Clark, Pete shifted in his seat as if he couldn't wait to have the assembly end.

"Hey, he's delivering an important message," Clark whispered to his friend.

"True, but the messenger is messed up," Pete whispered back.

". . . As my small contribution to show our unity against hate, I've taken the liberty of making Smallville flags of solidarity." Lex bent down and pulled a flag from the box at his feet and held it up to the crowd. In the center was an American flag, and surrounding it were brilliant stripes of every color in the rainbow.

"This flag represents our belief that Smallville

is open to people of all colors, all faiths, and all nations," Lex went on. "You'll find boxes of flags by the rear doors to the auditorium. As you leave this assembly, please take one with you, with my compliments. I hope you will fly your flag on your front lawn as proudly as I will fly mine."

Kids jumped to their feet to applaud him. Even Pete rose, albeit reluctantly, and put his hands together.

Shaaban, who was sitting on Clark's other side, applauded hardest of all. "Lex Luthor is a wonderful guy," he told Clark over the ovation.

Clark noticed two guys on the aisle, a couple of rows up, who weren't standing. In fact, they were slumped in their seats, arms folded. They both had buzz cuts. Clark couldn't see their faces.

Chloe was eyeing them, too. She nudged Shaaban.

"Who are they?" he asked her.

She shrugged. "Clark?"

"Must be upperclassmen," Clark guessed. "I'd need to get a look at them from the front."

Chloe thoughtfully tapped her bottom lip with

her finger. "Hmmm. I thought I knew everyone at this school."

Kids started to file out of the auditorium. Chloe peered around, trying to keep her eye on the two guys who hadn't stood up. They kept to themselves as they trudged out, hiding behind dark sunglasses.

"Well, we know it's not Deputy Melrose behind this," Chloe said. "You wanted me to find out where he was at the time of the attack? Handcuffed at the sheriff's office, where they were testing handcuffs!"

"Fine. It's not Melrose. But I don't like the looks of those two, whoever they are," Clark said, as Brian Parson, the son of Ms. Parson, sidled over.

"Those guys? I know 'em," Brian Parson said. He was in the same grade as Clark and Pete, and Clark thought he was a nice enough guy.

"So who are they?" Chloe demanded.

"Dennis Jones and Phil Richards. Moved here from Idaho a couple of months ago. I'm pretty sure they're seniors," Brian said.

"What's their deal?" Chloe pressed.

Brian shrugged. "Dennis has a little sister at the middle school. My mom's her teacher. I hear all the kids were home-schooled until they moved here."

"That doesn't mean a thing," Clark pointed out.

"They were the only ones who didn't give Lex a standing ovation," Shaaban said.

"I agree with Clark," Pete said. "Hey, maybe it was Ballister!"

"Right," Chloe snorted. "Our American History teacher snuck over to Shaaban's house and trashed it while no one was looking."

"If Shaaban had gotten a D on that last paper, I'd agree with Pete," Brian joked. "Anyway, I've got to get to class."

Pete nodded as Brian took off down the hall, Pete's sly smile belying his sincere tone. "Ballister. I could picture it."

"Don't even joke about that, Pete," Clark said.

"You guys, I will have more info on them by the time the last bell rings," Chloe promised them.

"You see, Clark, this is worthy of my time and brilliance. I'll catch you later. Rendezvous at the *Torch* office after school. Pass the word!" She zipped between moving bodies and disappeared into the crowd.

Shaaban watched her depart. "She's a very energetic girl."

Pete clapped him on the back. "You don't know the half of it, bro."

Clark excused himself and turned in the same direction as Dennis and Phil, tailing them as they wove through the teeming hallway. He knew that Pete had a grudge against Ballister — now that he thought about it, it seemed like Pete was harboring a lot of grudges, lately — but Clark felt certain that the teacher had nothing to do with vandalizing Shaaban's house.

When Dennis and Phil stopped at their lockers to stash some books, Clark noted their locker numbers.

He knew he'd be back.

CHAPTER 8

"Ladies and gentleman, the info diva has arrived as advertised," Chloe announced, as she strode into the school newspaper office ten minutes after school let out. Clark, Lana, Shaaban, and Tina were waiting for her.

"So, what else did you find out?" Clark asked. "Was Brian right about them?"

"Affirmative." Chloe hopped onto a table, legs dangling. "It seems their families are best friends, and the two families moved here together. The shorter one with the blond hair — that's Dennis. His parents split up a few months ago. Evidently, it was really ugly; hard on the kid. Anyway, he moved here with his mom and her new mega-bucks boyfriend. They bought one of those huge houses in the Luthorcorp subdivision. The other one, Phil, is a terrible student. Both guys list 'hunting' as a hobby."

"Wow," Tina exclaimed. "I am impressed. How'd you find all that out?"

"Pumped their guidance counselor," Chloe admitted. "I told her I was doing an article on new kids for the *Torch*, to introduce the school to them. I also offered to help her with filing during my free period; I snuck a peek at their records when she hit the john."

"Impressive," Shaaban admitted.

"You are too, too kind," Chloe said, sweeping her hand grandly and dropping her head in a regal bow.

"I admit all that sounds suspicious," Lana allowed, "but it doesn't mean they're the ones who wrecked Shaaban's house."

"Hey, they've got skinhead buzz cuts, they don't stand at the assembly, they're from Idaho — that's where all those crazed militia dudes are," Chloe ticked off.

"I didn't want to stand at the assembly, either," Pete reminded her.

"Chloe, what you're saying would not stand up in a court of law," Tina announced.

Pete shot her a look. "We're not *in* a court of law."

"You can never start planning your career path too early," Tina explained.

"I'll see what else I can find out," Clark offered. He went for casual, though he already knew exactly what he was going to do. "Not that I can match the efforts of Sleuth Girl, here," he added with a self-effacing grin.

"So, meeting adjourned?" Tina asked. "Because if I don't get home to finish my history paper, my grandmother is going to airmail me back to Singapore."

"Umm . . . we need to do some work on our African dance," Shaaban reminded them.

Clark and Pete groaned at the same time.

"I can't believe, Shaaban, with what your family went through, that you'd even still think about it," Lana said.

"It's good to keep busy," Shaaban admitted.

"Hey, we're all in it together," Chloe said. "Besides, what better way to show solidarity than with Shaaban and his parents?"

"And you guys will look so cute without shirts," Tina added sweetly.

"I'll go topless if you go topless," Pete offered.

Tina threw a paper wad at him.

Clark grasped at straws. "Maybe we could . . . I don't know . . . read an African poem or something. Wouldn't that be just as good?"

"No, it wouldn't," Lana told him. She gazed up at Clark. "Seriously. I think it's important for us to do this."

One long look from Lana was enough to melt Clark's resistance. "You're right," he agreed.

It's like those eyes are the only thing that I can't —

"Oh, Your Tallness?" Chloe called out, waving a hand in front of his eyes.

Clark blinked. "Sorry. What?"

"I said there's some more research we need to do at the library here. Want to go now?

I need some time alone first.

"How about if I meet you in an hour and a half?" he invented. "I need to go back to the farm and help my dad with some chores."

Chloe smiled, "Clark Kent, Future Farmer of America."

"And we can practice the dance after dinner tonight, in Clark's loft," Shaaban added. "Does that fit everyone's schedule? I'll bring the music. If we're lucky, my father will be around to demonstrate. The man has some moves."

It was a plan.

❧ ❧ ❧ ❧

His friends gone, the school hallways were empty. It was exactly the way Clark wanted it. He headed back to the newer wing, to Dennis's and Phil's lockers, and stood before them. He knew that he could rip the locks off, but that would leave them suspiciously open.

He fired his X-ray vision at the lockers. But it was useless. It seems these lockers had been repainted with lead-based paint a few years back. And his X-ray vision was useless through lead. That was a bad thing. But lead could also protect him against the deadly effects of the green meteorites.

That's a good thing, Clark thought. *Anyway, there's always another way.*

Simultaneously, using superhearing, he grasped the locks and swung both dials back and forth.

He heard the tumblers inside the lock clicking, and memorized the "sound" of the proper combinations.

And then, the two lockers popped open.

Quickly, Clark looked inside. There were the usual books and backpacks. But also hockey sticks and baseball bats.

They could use those as weapons, Clark thought. *Or they might just be into sports. Chloe probably already knows whether or not they play hockey and baseball.*

He poked around. Baseball gloves. More books. CDs. Books. And then, on the top shelf of Dennis's locker, a can of spray paint.

Clark inhaled sharply, remembering the paint that had defiled Shaaban's living room wall. The recollection made him so angry that he felt like putting his fist through Dennis's locker. He could have easily done it, too.

Then Clark took a close look at the can in the locker. It was blue, not the red of the hateful graffiti.

I can't accuse Dennis on the basis of a can of blue paint in his locker. I'll be watching him, though.

Because why would someone bring a can of spray paint to school?

※ ※ ※ ※

"So, what's the research we still have to do?" Clark asked Chloe later, when they were riding in her car.

"Something I read when we were at the Metropolis library has been bugging me, so I dug a little more, and . . ." She flicked her eyes at him, then back on the road. "Actually, we aren't going to the library. I just said that because everyone else was around."

"Why the mystery?"

"It has something to do with the attack on Shaaban's house, in a weird way," Chloe said. "But I'd really rather just show you."

Clark smiled and pointed to his fastened — but utterly pointless — seatbelt. "I'm a captive audience."

Twenty minutes later, they had tromped into the middle of a cornfield, just on the outskirts of Smallville.

"As far as I can figure out, this is it," Chloe announced.

Clark folded his arms. "You had to bring me out to a cornfield. And you couldn't tell anyone else. Of course, we are in Kansas. And Kansas has ten zillion cornfields. So this must be a double-top-secret cornfield."

"Spare me the sarcasm. Details are coming." She pulled a photocopied newspaper clipping from her pocket and handed it to Clark.

It was from an old edition of the Smallville *Ledger*. The article was dated December 16, 1941, with the dateline a day before. Clark read it in a millisecond.

HOME BURNS NEAR TOWN LIMITS

Smallville, Dec. 15. Last night, a fire destroyed the home of Yoshi Hiromura, a recent immigrant to Kansas. The home was burned to the ground and nothing of value remained. The Hiromura family has returned to San Francisco to live with relatives. Manfred Bikums, chief of the Smallville Fire Department, tells the *Ledger* that the fire evidently started when some rags in the barn combusted spontaneously. "By the time our engines got there, there was nothing left to save," Bikums said.

Clark handed the article back to Chloe. "There was a fire. The house burned. There's nothing left. There's corn here now." He looked around at the endless stalks bowing in the breeze, golden in the late afternoon light. "I mean, I know it's a tragedy, but it happened in nineteen forty-one. Even my parents weren't alive in nineteen forty-one. So why the field trip?"

"Think, Clark," she coaxed him, holding the article out to him again. "Look at the date."

Clark did. "December 15th, 1941."

"Doesn't that mean anything to you?"

"Why would that . . ." Clark's voice trailed off in mid-sentence. Because he suddenly understood. It was like a fist in his stomach, or how he imagined one would feel if he didn't have abs of steel.

"Pearl Harbor," he said. "The Japanese sneak attack on Pearl Harbor."

"Took place eight days before," Chloe finished for him. "Exactly."

Clark looked at the field, so benign-looking,

such an oasis of calm, and realized he must have passed it a thousand times in his life. It didn't look special in any way. And yet, something really significant might have happened there.

Dread crept up the back of his neck. "You're thinking what I'm thinking, Chloe, I know you are."

"Yeah."

"What if it wasn't an accident?"

Chloe nodded.

Clark thought aloud. "The family's name was Hiromura, which is a Japanese name. The fire was so bad that nothing was left of the home, forcing the family to move back to San Francisco . . ."

"And although the fire chief said it was an accident, it wouldn't be the first time that the powers that be in Smallville got the facts wrong," Chloe put in.

"If it was deliberately set, then the attack on the Mwariris isn't the first hate crime in Smallville, after all." With a determined stride, Clark headed into the tall corn.

"You and your endless legs," Chloe complained, trying to keep up. "Where are we going?"

"I want to find where the house used to be."

"Clark, it's a cornfield, you'll never —"

Suddenly, Clark stopped. He'd been sweeping the ground with his X-ray vision, looking for signs of the foundation.

And here it was, just below his feet. Concrete.

"This is the place," Clark announced. "I can feel it."

"Yuh," Chloe scoffed. "I know you're a country boy, but country boys are only supposed to be able to divine water, not cement."

Clark kicked at the topsoil, scuffing away the loamy earth. If he'd been alone, he could have burrowed down in an instant, but even in real time, it didn't take long before concrete appeared — the top of the Hiromura home's foundation.

Chloe whistled. "Will wonders never cease. You've got a career on *Law and Order*, if you want. Or maybe we should just set you up in a Vegas showroom."

"Right now there is only one thing I want," Clark said, "and that's to find out the truth about the hate crimes in Smallville." His eyes met Chloe's.

"I know it's just a generic small town to you. And I know you're going as far away to college as you can get. But Smallville is the only home I've ever known."

How could I possibly explain what it means to me, knowing that my home was once light years from this planet, but I can never go to that home again?

"Clark," Chloe reached for his hand, touched by the emotion in his voice.

"I love Smallville, Chloe. That this kind of stuff could go on here . . ."

"Hey, we're a team," she told him, giving him a luminous smile. "We'll find out the truth. Okay?"

He nodded. She reached way up to give him a quick hug.

"One other thing, Clark."

"What?"

"It's not a generic small town to me. Not as long as people I love are here."

Clark knew, without Chloe's saying it, that one of those people was him.

CHAPTER 9

Clark lay in his sleeping bag, listening to the steady, deep breathing of his friend Shaaban in the sleeping bag across the loft. Clark was amazed that Shaaban had actually been able to fall asleep. Maybe it was the African dance they'd rehearsed that had made it possible. Shaaban had brought over a large Tanzanian drum that, fortunately, hadn't been damaged in the attack on their home. He demonstrated some basic steps for them, and then beat out a rhythm for their dance.

Shaaban explained that the dance was about community and harmony, both with neighbors and with a special someone. Clark was bad at it, and Pete was worse. But at least they learned they wouldn't have to wear embarrassing costumes on the coming Sunday. Dr. Mwariri was loaning them dashikis for the occasion — loose, colorful tunics.

Clark glanced at the clock. It was almost three o'clock in the morning. He'd been tossing and turning for hours. In fact, he'd had the most terrible nightmare, dreaming he'd been in a house that was burning up. Normally, with his superpowers, he could walk through the flames, untouched and unharmed.

But in this dream, the flames weren't red. They were green, fueled by chunks of the only thing that could weaken Clark — the greenish meteorites that had fallen to Earth along with his spaceship. Clark had felt the air punched out of his lungs by the lethal heat, seen his veins writhe under his skin like a dozen black anacondas, watched from outside of himself as he crumpled to the white-hot ground, gasping, screaming, dying.

He'd sat up with a gasp, drenched in sweat.

It was the Hiromura house, Clark realized the moment he was awake. *That's what gave me such a terrible nightmare.*

But identifying the source of the nightmare didn't make getting back to sleep any easier. When he closed his eyes, all he could see were the red letters that had been spray-painted on the wall of Shaaban's home.

GO BACK TO AFREAKA!

Clark lay there restlessly a little while longer, and then decided to go and get something to eat. Not because he was so hungry but because it would give him something to do. He pulled on a sweatshirt and some jeans, then padded out of the loft and over to the main farmhouse.

To his surprise, the lights were on in the kitchen. And when he came in the door, his dad was at the kitchen table, reading the *Ledger* and nibbling on some of Martha's homemade peanut-butter and pecan cookies.

Clark was glad to see him. Jonathan had spent the day at a Department of Agriculture seminar in Metropolis, and hadn't gotten home by the time Clark and Shaaban had turned in for the night.

Jonathan smiled wanly when Clark came

through the kitchen door. "You couldn't sleep either, huh?"

"I had the worst nightmare," Clark admitted, pouring a glass of milk. He sat across from his dad. "I was caught in a fire made from those green meteors and I was dying."

Jonathan pushed the plate of cookies toward his son. "Your mom's cookies can cure pretty much anything. At least you thought so when you were a kid."

Clark bit into one. "How long have you been awake?"

Jonathan shook his head. "Since I supposedly went to bed. All I can think about is catching the jerk who trashed the Mwariris' house. I'm not sure that Wayne Melrose is quite up to the job."

"I thought you said he was a good deputy."

"He called yesterday and left a message that he wants to interview you again," Jonathan said to his son. "He seems to think that you and your friends had something to do with the vandalism."

Clark made a noise of disgust. "Great. Like *that* makes any sense."

"I informed him that he was very much barking up the wrong tree." Jonathan stared thoughtfully into his glass. "Who would do something like this, Clark? I keep asking myself that. I know I sound like a broken record —"

"No one has records anymore, Dad," Clark pointed out.

"Thank you for calling my age to my attention," his father added dryly. "What I meant was, the same sentence just keeps playing over and over in my mind: 'I just can't believe this could happen in Smallville.'"

"I can't, either." Clark took a long gulp of milk. "I guess I don't want to believe that anyone in Smallville is carrying that much hate."

Jonathan polished off another cookie. "This town has always been special. Did you know that before the Civil War, Kansas was one of the states that allowed slavery? But there wasn't a single slave-holding family here in Smallville."

"I didn't know that," Clark said. "But it's great."

"Or that a relative of your friend Pete was one of the first black mayors elected in any American town where the population majority was white? This was back in the early sixties."

"Pete has mentioned it once or twenty times," Clark said with a grin.

"My point is, son, just because a town is small doesn't mean it's backwards. Nothing like what the Mwariris are going through has ever happened here before."

"I'm not sure that's true, Dad."

His father looked quizzically at Clark.

"Did you ever hear of the Hiromura family?" Clark asked.

Jonathan shook his head, so Clark filled him in on everything that he'd learned about the Japanese family whose home had burned to the ground.

"The fire chief called it an accident," Clark concluded, "but I've got major doubts about that. You've never even heard anyone mention this? Not even when you were a kid?"

"I know you think I'm ancient, but I was born a long time after that happened. I never heard my parents talk about it, either."

"It was just after Pearl Harbor," Clark said. "I have this feeling it wasn't an accident."

Jonathan gave a low whistle. "This is one case where I hope you're wrong."

"Me, too. But I have to find out the truth, Dad. If what happened to the Hiromuras was deliberate, and someone tried to burn them out because they were Japanese, we can't just bury it under the rug."

Jonathan ran a hand through his hair. "There's a lot to be proud of about America," he finally said. "But there are some things to be ashamed of, too. How our government and our people treated Japanese Americans during World War II is one of them."

"We don't study it in school," Clark said. "No one talks about it. How are we ever supposed to do better if we don't know the bad things we did in the past?"

Jonathan sighed. "People tend not to want to shine light on the dark places, Clark. It's just human nature."

Clark set his jaw. "Maybe. But not mine." He took his glass to the sink and rinsed it out. "I want to find out who attacked the Mwariris. And if the fire at the Hiromura place in 1941 was a hate crime, I want to find that out, too."

Jonathan pursed his lips. "It won't be easy. I told you, people would rather let sleeping dogs lie."

"But I know you don't feel that way," Clark insisted. "And I'm sure Mom doesn't."

"You're right," his father agreed.

"What if the 'good old days' had just as many problems and just as much hate?" Clark went on. "I mean, unless we find out and face up to it, we'll just end up repeating it."

"I know that, Clark. I told you, I agree with you. I'm only saying that there may be people who don't."

"The truth will set you free." That's what Lana told me, even if she couldn't bring herself to carry it out the other day, he recalled. *I know this much: Lana is right.*

"Chloe and I are going to dig as deep as we have to dig to find out the truth," Clark insisted.

Jonathan smiled. "I had a feeling you were going to say that."

"You did?"

"That's the kind of person you are." He took his glass to the sink. "I just want you to know, Clark, that no matter what you find out, your Mom and I are with you on this one hundred percent."

Clark felt a lump in his throat.

My dad can be tough on me, sometimes. And he can be strict. But when it comes to what's right and what's wrong, he's all about what's right.

"Thanks, Dad. That means a lot to me."

His father smiled sadly. "You're such a good person, Clark. Too often, it's the good people who get hurt."

"The good people are the ones I'm here to help," Clark said with quiet authority. "I don't understand why there has to be evil. But I don't believe it's stronger than the forces of good."

"Your mom tends to be a lot more philosophical about this stuff than I do, son. But maybe . . . well, maybe you can't have love in the world if you don't have hate, too."

"Maybe not in any world," Clark murmured.

His father looked at him quizzically.

"Sometimes I wonder what happened in . . . wherever it is I came from," Clark explained. "Did the planet I lived on blow up in some terrible war? Did hate kill off everyone and everything? . . ." He couldn't go on. It was just too painful.

Jonathan put his hand on top of his son's. "I wish I had answers for you, Clark, but I don't. What I do know is this: This is *your* world, now. And having you in it makes it a much better place for everyone."

CHAPTER 10

After school the next day, Lana and Chloe were already in the *Torch* office when Clark arrived. He and Chloe had done research during their free period that day, trying to find out more about the Hiromura family, and Lana was meeting them to get a progress report. They were due to meet Tina and Pete later at Tina's house to finalize the plans for the Multicultural Day performances.

"There you are, Clark. I almost started without you," Chloe said.

Lana shook her head. "This whole thing is really upsetting. I asked Nell, and she's never even heard of the Hiromura family. What did you two find out?"

"We actually dug up an article about them in

an old issue of the *Torch* from 1938," Clark told her, taking a copy of the article from his notebook. He handed it to Lana.

"The Hiromuras moved to Smallville that year from California. They bought a farmhouse just outside of town," Chloe added.

"Mr. Hiromura was born in the United States; his wife was an immigrant from Kyoto, Japan," Clark said. "They had two children. One of them, a daughter named Joellen, attended Smallville High that year."

"And then her home burned down," Lana said sadly. Accompanying the article was a photo of Joellen. She had long, dark hair and a petite frame. She was all dressed up for her picture, with a hopeful smile on her face. Lana handed the article back to Clark.

The photo is grainy and the details are blurred, but I think Joellen looks kind of like Lana, Clark ruminated.

It made the tragedy that much more tragic to him.

"If she's still alive she must be, what, nearly

eighty now," Chloe calculated. "What I can't figure out is why no one ever talks about this. I mean, there are plenty of people in the area who would have been alive then."

"If they figured it was an accident, then I guess it wouldn't stand out in their mind," Lana suggested.

"Hey, how's it going?" Brian Parson said as he walked into the office. "I didn't think you'd be here, Chloe. I was just going to drop off my review of the new *Birds of Prey* Web site." He handed Chloe a few sheets of paper.

"Thanks, Brian. Right on time." Chloe stuck the article in her "In" box.

"No prob." Brian headed back toward the door, and then turned back to them. "Listen, I thought you guys might be interested, for what it's worth . . ."

"What?" Chloe asked.

"Dennis Jones came up to me at lunch and asked me if I could tutor him in math — somebody recommended me to him."

"Is there more?" Chloe asked, clearly anxious to get back to their meeting.

Brian shrugged. "Only that he starts telling me how the minorities wreck everything and take up all the teachers' time, and that's why a guy like him has to hire a tutor."

"What a jerk," Lana seethed.

"Yeah, well . . . with Multicultural Day coming and all that, I thought you might want to know. Anyway, I'll be at the library with him tonight, in case you need to check him out. See you."

"I'm on it," Clark assured his friends as Brian left. He wasn't about to tell them what he'd seen in Dennis's locker, because he had no explanation for how he could have seen it.

"What are you going to do?" Lana asked. "You can't ask the kid if he and his idiot friend trashed the Mwariri house."

"I'll think of something," Clark said evasively.

"This whole thing makes me feel so powerless," Lana said. "I just want to *do* something . . ." A thoughtful look came over her face. "Wait. Maybe we can."

"I can see the wheels of brilliance turning," Pete said.

Lana checked her watch. "We have an hour

before we're supposed to meet at Tina's house. I was thinking we could take boxes of those flags that Lex had made, and go door to door with them on the way. For people who don't already have one."

"It's your inner Betsy Ross," Chloe said sweetly. "Anyway, count me in."

Everyone else agreed, too, except Clark. "I'll meet you guys at Tina's," he said. "There's something I need to do first."

"You're such a mysterious boy," Chloe teased, eyeing him flirtatiously.

"Oh, I don't know," Lana said. "I think Clark's pretty straightforward."

Chloe wiggled her eyebrows. "I always say that still waters run deep."

Lana smiled. "I know he's deep. But I also know that the guy I see is the guy he is. I would call Clark Kent pretty much the most honest, straightforward person I know. Right, Clark?"

Wait a sec. Are they fighting *over me?*

"Uh . . ." Clark couldn't think of a single thing to say.

"Succinctly put, Clark." Chloe patted him on the arm and slid off the table, looping her backpack over one arm. "Lana and I may have to be like King Solomon and cut you in half."

"I'm not after Clark," Lana told Chloe. "I have a boyfriend. Just because Whitney's away in the Marines doesn't mean we're not still together."

"Uh-*huh!*" Chloe chirped.

Clark knew that too-too-happy tone of Chloe's only too-too well. It meant that Chloe didn't believe Lana at all.

CHAPTER 11

Clark trudged down the street, fighting the impulse simply to super-speed to Tina's. But he didn't dare — there were too many cars on the road. He knew how weird it would look to a casual observer if one instant he were there and the next instant, gone.

"Protect your secret, Clark." He didn't know how many times his mom and dad had told him that. But it was a lot.

And there've been plenty of times when I've almost blown it, Clark thought. *Like just a few minutes ago.*

After the others left to go on their flag giveaway, he'd returned to Dennis's and Phil's lockers to check them out again. Again, he'd opened them surreptitiously. But just as he was about to look inside, Principal Reynolds had come around the corner.

He did manage, though, to sneak a quick peek inside Dennis's locker before he closed it. Now there were *two* cans of spray paint on the top shelf. But again, neither of them was red. Clark had left school with his suspicions further aroused.

Clark kept plodding along. So many of the homes he passed had solidarity flags in their windows or on their front lawns. It made him feel good. Ten minutes later Clark turned onto Tina's block — cul-de-sac, actually. Even walking slowly, he knew he'd arrive at Tina's house ahead of everyone else.

He'd been there several times. The house was white, surrounded by gardens that were the pride and joy of Tina's grandmother, and was at the crest of what passed in Kansas for a hill. Its backyard sloped down to the next street. Clark remembered old Mrs. Wu complaining about how the house was always cold, which is why he chuckled when a massive heating oil truck rumbled past him.

I'd bet money that truck's heading for —

Clark inhaled sharply. Instead of slowing to a stop in front of Tina's house, the truck was bearing down directly on the home.

Did the driver pass out? If the truck hits the house . . .

But he had no time to think, no time to consider whether anyone would see what he was about to do. He churned his legs in an amazing burst of speed, going into Clark time. Although in real life the truck was moving, in Clark time the vehicle appeared to be frozen. Clark took a mighty leap up and through the driver's side window. Razor-sharp glass shards flew in all directions.

Now out of Clark time, Clark couldn't believe his eyes. There was no one driving, and a wooden board was jammed against the accelerator, holding it to the floor. Clark cut the steering wheel to the left, slammed on the brakes with one foot, and smashed the other one down against the board, busting it to smithereens.

The stuck accelerator released and the truck

skidded wildly, barreling over the curb and onto the Wus' lawn, through one of grandmother Wu's prized gardens, nearly sideswiping the house in the process.

Finally, Clark wrestled the vehicle to a stop at the top of the embankment. He breathed a sigh of relief. Below him, he could see homes. If the truck had barreled over the hill, those homes would now be completely ablaze.

"Hey, you! You in the truck!"

Did someone see me? I have to think of an excuse, a reasonable explanation. Think, brain, think!

Clark opened the driver's side door and stepped out. Many of the cul-de-sac's residents were on the street now, with more gathering every second. Clark's friends had just turned onto the cul-de-sac, and they came running when they saw the skid marks of the truck across the lawn.

"Hey, you in the truck!" Pushing through the throng was the uniformed gas truck driver. He grabbed Clark's hand and pumped it. "Thank God. Thank God for you, son! How the heck did you stop it?"

"It wasn't going that fast," Clark invented, "so I managed to jump on. I guess I was in the right place at the right time."

Lana shouldered in next to the driver. "Clark, are you okay?"

Clark brushed some glass shards from his shoulders. "Fine, I think."

"It's a wonder you weren't killed," she said, concern etched between her eyes.

"I'm okay," Clark insisted.

As people babbled to the truck driver, the rest of Clark's friends crowded in around Clark.

"Man, if we had footage, you would *so* be on the national news," Pete said. "Unreal."

Well, thank God we don't have footage, Clark thought.

"You amaze me, Clark," Chloe marveled. "You so often seem to be the one who saves someone or something from disaster."

"I don't know if that makes me lucky or unlucky," Clark said ruefully. It was the best response he could think of.

"Well, it certainly makes Smallville lucky," Tina said.

"I'm just glad I could help," Clark said. He turned to the truck driver. "This is your truck, right?"

The driver nodded. "Everybody keeps asking me what happened, and I don't even know. One minute I'm turning onto this street, everything normal, the next, I'm outside the truck, on the ground, and it's rolling away from me."

"You don't remember getting out of the truck?" Clark asked.

"No," the driver said. "Because I didn't get out of the truck."

"Maybe he's been drinking," someone in the crowd called out.

"Hey, I got twenty years on the job and never had a problem," the driver insisted. "And I never took a drink in my life. I'm telling you, this is freaky!"

"There was a wooden plank holding down the accelerator," Clark said. "You didn't do that?"

The driver looked aghast. "Are you kidding?"

It was obvious to Clark that the guy was telling the truth.

"I called the cops," a woman in the crowd informed them. "They're on their way."

"Where's the board you were talking about, Clark?" Chloe asked, peering into the truck. "The sheriff will want to see it."

"Oh, I, uh, managed to smash my heel through it."

Chloe plucked up a sliver of wood. "You mean this? There's tons of 'em in the cab. How could the heel of your sneaker do that?"

"It must have been . . . really flimsy pressboard," Clark said. To his relief, Chloe seemed to buy his explanation.

I'm lucky no one saw me use my powers. I hope Chloe doesn't look too deeply into the wooden plank thing, because it sure wasn't flimsy wood. It looked like it came from a fence . . .

Clark looked around, his gaze fixing on a building site at the entrance to the cul-de-sac, where a new home was under construction.

That's where the board came from. I'm sure of it.

Now he felt more concerned than ever that something really awful was going on in Smallville, and that this was no accident.

He pulled Chloe aside. "There's a big problem

here. First, the flyers for Multicultural Day are set on fire. Then, Shaaban's house is trashed. Now, an oil truck is rigged to plow into Tina's home. I think it's all connected, Chloe."

"You think someone was targeting the Wus," Chloe asked him quietly, so that no one else could hear, "because they're Asian?"

"I don't want to think so," Clark replied, "but I do."

Chloe folded her arms. "So do I."

Clark was careful to keep his voice down. "If we're right, Chloe, a lot of people are in danger. The first attack was petty arson, the second was against property, and thank God no one was home just now. The next time could be . . ."

He didn't need to finish the sentence for Chloe to understand.

The next time, it could be murder.

CHAPTER 12

Genesis Journal, Entry #2

UNREAL. MY POWERS CONTINUE TO GROW.

I MADE A LIST OF THE OTHERS WHO I MUST DRIVE FROM SMALLVILLE. THE NEXT NAME ON MY LIST WAS WU. THE GIRL, TINA, IS AN HONORS STUDENT AT SMALLVILLE HIGH. I'M SURE THE FAMILY PLANS ON HER GETTING A SCHOLARSHIP TO SOME EXPENSIVE COLLEGE, TAKING UP A SPOT THAT BELONGS TO A <u>REAL</u> AMERICAN. WELL, I COULD DO SOMETHING ABOUT THAT INJUSTICE. AND I WOULD.

I CASED THE WU HOUSE AHEAD OF TIME. I PLANNED TO DO IT AFTER SCHOOL. WHEN I GOT HOME, I HEARD MY MOTHER IN THE KITCHEN PRACTICING

Spanish with a tape. She says it will be helpful, because more and more Spanish-speaking people are moving to Smallville.

I gagged. My dad says that in the old days, people in Smallville only learned Spanish if they were forced to take it in high school. Now, even some farmers are learning Spanish so they can talk with their migrant workers. And some of the migrant workers aren't migrating anymore. They decided they liked Smallville, so they settled down here. One of these days, the majority of people in Smallville won't be white anymore. Wake up, you stupid morons of civilization! While you're holding hands and singing "Kumbayah" and embracing "cultural diversity," the Others are taking over.

What was even worse was that one of those Solidarity Flags was up on our front door. My own front door! What if my dad showed up and saw it? That about sent me into a full-on Reds attack.

I PULLED OFF THE FLAG AND RAN TO MY ROOM, WHERE I RIPPED IT AND RIPPED IT AND RIPPED IT INTO RAGS. THAT HELPED ME COME DOWN FROM THE REDS. THEN I FLIPPED THE HOURGLASS, AND PASSED INTO THE ZONE.

I CASUALLY STROLLED OVER TO TINA'S HOUSE, ENJOYING THE FROZEN WORLD AROUND ME. I PASSED A COUPLE OF CHEERLEADERS ABOUT TO GET INTO A JEEP WITH THEIR BOYFRIENDS. JUST BECAUSE THEY'RE HOTTIES, THOSE GIRLS THINK THEY CAN GET AWAY WITH ANYTHING. THEY NEVER LOOK AT A GUY LIKE ME. I WENT OVER TO THEM, SASHAYED AROUND, ADMIRING THE SCENERY, SO TO SPEAK. IN NORMAL TIME, THEY WOULD HAVE TOLD ME TO GET LOST; THEIR BOYFRIENDS WOULD HAVE KICKED MY BUTT. BUT NOW, THEY COULDN'T DO ANY-THING TO STOP ME. IT WAS AWESOME, AMAZING. I COULD HAVE DONE ANYTHING I WANTED. ANYTHING.

BUT AS I SAID IN AN EARLIER ENTRY, THAT IS NOT THE WAY MY FATHER RAISED ME. DON'T CHEAT, DON'T STEAL, TREAT

PEOPLE WHO ARE YOUR EQUAL WITH
RESPECT. SO NO WAY WAS I GOING TO
DISRESPECT THOSE CHEERLEADERS. MY
DAD ALWAYS TREATED MY MOTHER GREAT.
AND WHAT DID SHE DO? BYE, BYE, MISS
AMERICAN PIE. REPLACED MY DAD WITH <u>HIM.</u>
AND NOW, THERE'S A RESTRAINING ORDER
ON MY DAD TO PREVENT HIM FROM SEEING
ME. HOW FAIR IS THAT?

JUST THE THOUGHT OF IT MAKES ME
FEEL RED.

RED, RED, RED, RED . . . .

OKAY. I'M CALMER NOW. TALKED THE
REDS DOWN. SOMETIMES I CAN DO THAT.

THIS MONSTER OIL TRUCK WAS GOING INTO
THE CUL-DE-SAC. WHEN I SAW THAT, A
HUGE GRIN SPREAD OVER MY FACE. OH MAN,
WHAT I COULD DO WITH THAT. I
OPENED THE DOOR OF THE FROZEN TRUCK
AND PULLED THE DRIVER OUT. HE FELT
LIKE DEAD WEIGHT, BUT FORTUNATELY HE
WASN'T THAT BIG OF A GUY.

I LOOKED AROUND FOR SOMETHING TO
ASSIST ME IN MY PLAN. AT A CONSTRUC-
TION SITE WAS A PILE OF PLANKS. SO I
GRABBED ONE AND CLIMBED BACK INTO THE

OIL TRUCK. THEN I WEDGED THE WOODEN
PLANK IN SUCH A WAY THAT THE GAS
PEDAL WOULD STAY PRESSED DOWN,
WHICH WOULD MAKE THE DRIVERLESS TRUCK
PICK UP SPEED AND HEAD STRAIGHT INTO
THE WU HOUSE.

I KNEW MY TWO HOURS HAD TO BE AL-
MOST UP, MY TIME IN THE ZONE NEARLY
OVER. EXCITED TO WATCH THE FRUITS OF
MY GENIUS, I HID BEHIND THE HOUSE
NEXT DOOR TO THE WUS' AND WAITED
FOR THE SHOW TO BEGIN. BUT THEN —

CRAP. MY MOTHER JUST KNOCKED ON
MY DOOR. SHE'S ASKING IF I KNOW WHAT
HAPPENED TO THE FLAG FROM THE FRONT
DOOR. MORE LATER.

CHAPTER 13

Lex was behind his desk in his opulent home office, going over some papers with Ms. Parson, when a servant showed Clark into the room.

Lex rose and shook Clark's hand. "Clark, my friend. Always good to see you."

"Good morning, Clark," Ms. Parson said with a warm smile.

"Good morning." He turned to Lex. "I appreciate you seeing me on such short notice, but I can see that I'm interrupting —"

"Nonsense," Lex said. "Just a few last-minute details for our festival. Ms. Parson has an excellent handle on it. In light of recent events, it couldn't be more appropriate."

"Thanks, Mr. Luthor, I appreciate your faith in me." She rose and stuck the papers into her briefcase. "So, Clark, how's the African dance coming along?"

"It's really . . . African," Clark said lamely.

"I'm sure it will be wonderful," Ms. Parson said. "After what the Mwariris went through . . ." She shook her head and sighed. "Well, I just feel that it's more important than ever to make sure they feel like a part of this community."

"I couldn't agree with you more," Lex said.

"There are so many good people in this town," Ms. Parson said. "I know we'll stand together against hate. I'll see myself out, Mr. Luthor." She headed out the door.

"Nice woman," Lex opined, folding his arms. "So, Clark, my friend, have a seat."

"Thanks." Clark sat on the buttery leather sofa.

"Can I get you some breakfast? Coffee? A beverage, perhaps?"

"No, thanks. My mother made pancakes. Not that I ate any."

"Too much on your mind, eh?" Lex guessed. "I heard about your exploits yesterday. They're lucky you were able to stop that truck. I understand it was quite the heroic effort."

"Not really," Clark demurred.

"Always so modest, Clark. Is that what you came to talk with me about?"

"No. It's something else." Clark couldn't figure out how to broach the subject, so he just plowed into it. "It's really shameful how some people treated Japanese Americans during the Second World War."

Lex laughed. "I have come to expect the unexpected from you, Clark, but that's still quite the non sequitur."

"Do you know what happened back then?" Clark asked.

"Tule Lake, Minidoka, Manzanar," Lex rattled off, ticking the strange names off on the fingers of his right hand as he did.

"What are those?"

"The names of some of the internment camps out west," Lex explained. "Places where our government sent American citizens of Japanese ancestry during the war. The Supreme Court approved it. *Korematsu* v. *United States*, I think."

Lex pushed a button on his desk, and a floor-to-ceiling map of the United States descended from a recessed panel. Lex got up from his desk, grabbed a pool stick from the rack on the wall, and pointed to various locations on the map. "They were here, here, and here."

Clark nodded thoughtfully. "How do you know all that?"

Lex smiled thinly. "Once I realized that my learning curve wasn't going to thrive in a classroom setting, I began to teach myself about the things that are really important." He gestured to the map. "Power. Abuse of power. Pride and prejudice. I suppose you could say these were my majors."

"Because of your father?" Clark ventured.

"In the sense that he could write the book on abuse of power, yes." Lex slid the billiards cue back into its holder. "In the sense that I ever intended to be anything like him, no."

"I know that —" Clark began.

Lex held a palm up. "It's fine, Clark. The truth is, I have a special interest in the subject."

"So do I," Clark said grimly.

Lex cocked his head at Clark. "Hmmm. Curious. At the risk of making this Show Off My Toys Day, let me show you something else."

Lex went back to his desk and pressed various buttons on the recessed console. The map retracted upward into the ceiling as two bookcases slid open. Behind them were a television monitor, a VCR/DVD player, and several shelves of tapes and DVDs. Clark waited while Lex hunted through the tapes until he found what he wanted.

"*Voila*," he said, popping one into the player. "Actually, I'm surprised I haven't already shared this with you, Clark. This is from five years ago."

A videotaped segment of a newscast lit up the TV screen. A crisp female reporter was doing a stand-up in front of a government building. "We're here at police headquarters in Brader Beach, Florida," she said. "The Brader Beach chief of police, Gary Gentry, is about to make a public statement regarding last night's arrest of seventeen-year-old Lex Luthor, son of the well-known industrialist Lionel Luthor."

"You were arrested?" Clark asked.

Lex put a finger to his lips.

Clark watched, astonished, as the camera cut to a microphone-festooned podium that had been placed at the top of the steps to the police station. Behind the podium were the police chief, young Lex, and Lionel Luthor himself. The grim-faced police chief took a prepared statement from his vest pocket, then cleared his throat and began to read the statement aloud.

"The police department and the community of Brader Beach issue this sincere apology to Mr. Lionel Luthor and his son, Lex Luthor, regarding the arrest of Lex Luthor last night on the beach." His eyes flicked up at the gathered reporters and then went back to his statement.

"Yesterday evening," he continued, "there was an incident on the beach where an African-American couple was attacked by a group of white skinheads. Lex Luthor intervened to try to prevent these skinheads from further injuring the couple. When the police responded, they mistakenly identified Lex Luthor as one of the perpetrators of the crime."

Behind the chief, Lionel Luthor offered an almost imperceptible nod. As for Lex, his jaw was set hard, his eyes flinty.

The chief continued. "Due to Lex Luthor's all-over baldness, rare for a young man of his age, the responding officers assumed that he was one of the skinhead perpetrators. Nothing could be further from the truth. I called this press conference to set the record straight, and to offer Mr. Luthor and his son, Lex, our most sincere apology."

Reporters began yelling out questions, but the chief stepped away from the microphone, and Lex came forward.

"I appreciate Chief Gentry's apology," he began. "However, I want the people of Brader Beach, and everyone else listening, to know that the mistake the police made when they arrested me last night is inexcusable."

The reporters began to fire questions at him, but Lex quieted them with a wave of his hand. "The police made an assumption about me based on my appearance. Their assumption was not the truth. If we can stop judging people by the color

of their skin, the clothes they wear, their hair —
or their lack of it — this world will be a much
better place for all of us."

The screen went black, as Lex clicked it off and
smiled at Clark. "I do sound a little pompous, I
know. But I was seventeen and I was very angry.
I'm sure you can see why."

"I thought you handled it really well, Lex,"
Clark told him. "I'm impressed."

Lex reached into the mini-fridge for a blue bottle of his favorite spring water. "Do you know
what my father said to me afterward?"

"What?"

"He said that I had used poor judgment in trying to stop the skinheads," Lex unscrewed the
top and took a long swallow.

"What does he expect you to do in the face of
evil? Nothing?"

"His concern was that I took on five men by
myself without a weapon of any kind," Lex explained. "When it comes to the art of war, Lionel
Luthor is the ultimate pragmatist. Anyway, it's
just this sort of experience that led to my interest

in battling prejudice. Because, in my own way, I've experienced it."

Clark looked at his watch. Unless he supersped to school, he'd be late. But what he'd come for was too important for him to leave now. "Lex, I need your help. It's kind of related to what you're talking about."

Lex leaned on the arm of the couch. "I'm all ears."

Clark quickly outlined everything that he'd learned about the fire that had burnt down the Hiromura home back in 1941, including his suspicions that although the official investigation had labeled it an accident, it was actually arson.

Lex drummed his fingers. "So, you think that the attack on the Mwariri home wasn't the first hate crime in Smallville. Interesting."

Clark nodded. "I was hoping maybe you could help Chloe and me get to the bottom of it."

Lex's face was tight. "It never stops, does it?"

"What never stops?"

"The fear of anyone different."

"I guess not," Clark agreed. "The other day

Lana told me that the truth sets you free. She was talking about something else, but it still applies. We have to find out the truth about what happened, even if it's unpleasant."

Lex downed the last of his water and set the bottle on his desk. "I'll walk you to the door. You're already late for school."

He didn't say whether or not he'd help me, Clark realized as they headed down the cavernous hallway.

"I'm glad I showed you that tape, Clark," Lex mused aloud as they approached the front door. "You've heard me say more than once that I don't like to get the police involved in things. Now you understand a little bit why I don't trust them very much."

"Yes. I understand," Clark said.

"I knew you would." Lex clapped Clark on the back. "That experience in Florida affected me a lot. I was in jail overnight. When I tried to tell the cops who I was, they wouldn't believe me. It wasn't until my father and an army of lawyers from Metropolis showed up that I got sprung. If I hadn't been Lionel Luthor's son, I could be in prison right now."

"Scary thought, huh?" Clark said quietly.

Lex nodded. "There's nothing I loathe more than prejudice, Clark. Nothing. I'll fight it every chance I get. If that pits me against the whole world, so be it." He held out his hand to Clark. "I'll help you any way I can."

Clark shook it gratefully. "Thanks."

"Call tomorrow afternoon," Lex instructed him. "I might have some information."

Clark was taken aback. "So fast?"

"When my friend Clark Kent asks me for a favor, it goes right to the top of my list."

It's a good thing Lex is one of the good guys, Clark thought, as he took in Lex's mirthless grin. *Because if he ever went to the dark side, he'd be one formidable villain.*

CHAPTER 14

"Hopefully, it won't take too long to turn us into passable African dancers," Clark told Chloe as she parked in front of his farmhouse. "We can go to Dennis's house afterwards. I want to see if he has an alibi for the attack at Shaaban's."

"Ringing the front door and asking him doesn't strike me as a plan," Chloe teased.

"Right, I know that," he said with a smile.

She laughed as they headed to Clark's loft for an African dance lesson with Dr. Mwariri. "I have a feeling they're the guys, Clark. I really do."

"But how did they do it?" Clark asked.

"As much as I hate to admit it, I'm clueless," Chloe said. "The time thing is wigging me out. How can two guys destroy an entire house in a matter of seconds with someone in the backyard, and that someone doesn't see them or hear them?"

"I don't know," Clark admitted. "It's as if time froze or something."

She comically batted her eyelashes. "Why, Clark, that's so woo-woo of you. And I mean that in the nicest possible way."

A few moments later, they were up in the loft, and Dr. Mwariri was telling them they were the last to arrive. Almost immediately, he started a rhythm on his big drum. "So, as I understand it, you young people have practiced twice with my son," Dr. Mwariri said, drumming as he talked.

There were nods all around.

"In our country, dance can express many things. It builds bridges between the wisdom of the elders and the young who are just finding their way. Shaaban told me that he has already introduced you to some simple and basic African dance movements."

"They didn't seem so simple to me," Pete muttered.

"I assure you, Pete, once the rhythm enters

your soul, your being will be infused with the power of the dance."

"In other words, you have to feel it," Shaaban said.

His father nodded. "The dance I will teach you is called the dance of Truth. In this dance, each of us expresses the truth of our hearts, and we are elevated by the joy and freedom of self-expression."

Pete looked highly dubious. "Okay, no offense, sir, but I have no idea what you're talking about."

"Honesty is a fine quality, Pete," Dr. Mwariri said. "Shaaban, do the drumming, please."

Shaaban wrapped the thick rope of the drum around his neck and began a steady, syncopated beat. His father combined the two moves that Shaaban had already taught them. One indicates love of community — the palms of the hands face outward and pulse on each beat. The other indicates romantic love of another person — the palms face inward, as if drawing the loved one closer. After that, Dr. Mwariri explained that they'd form a circle and do free movements, dancing inward until they all touched. They'd be individuals, yet dancing as one.

"That doesn't look too difficult," Chloe said, jumping to her feet. She reached down for Pete and hauled him up. "Come on. It's for a good cause."

Pete sighed. "That's what I keep telling myself."

Shaaban began drumming again. The beat was infectious. Dr. Mwariri encouraged them all to move freely to the music. Clark felt ridiculous at first, but after a while, he relaxed and started to get into it.

"This really isn't all that different from dancing to hip-hop at a party," Tina pointed out. "It's fun."

"Excellent!" Dr. Mwariri called to them. "Add hand movements."

The whole group loosened up, dancing around the loft, hands pulsing with palms outward, then switching to palms inward. "Hey, I think I'm getting the hang of this," Pete said as he bopped around the floor.

"Looking good, man!" Shaaban called to him.

The group made a circle dancing toward each other, tighter and tighter, until they danced together in one tight knot.

"I love this!" Chloe cried.

"Everyone loves the dance of Truth," Dr. Mwariri said. "Truth is joy."

Clark shimmied over toward Lana and let his palms pulse forward and backward, toward her and away from her. She noticed, and returned the gesture. The two of them grinned hugely. It really was fun.

Shaaban brought the drumming to an end in an impressive syncopated flourish; the group stopped and applauded him.

He took a mock bow. "You are too kind, my friends."

"As long as we don't wear stupid clothes, I am down for this," Pete said, a grin spreading across his face.

"Your dashiki will be highly appropriate and not at all stupid," Shaaban assured him.

They practiced the dance one more time, and then the group broke up, feeling reasonably confident about their performance for Sunday. Shaaban and Pete planned to go home with Tina to study at Tina's house.

But I can't go with them to make sure they're safe, Clark thought.

"Are you sure that's what you want to do?" he asked, thinking about their safety. "You can study here, you know."

"My grandmother baked," Tina explained. "She's expecting us. Besides, she called upon all our ancestors to rise up and vanquish anyone who tries to mess with the Wus, or anyone under the Wu roof," Tina informed him. "In other words, she'll be insulted if we *don't* study at my house. Anyway, Mr. Luthor put security guards at the entrance to our cul-de-sac and in front of the house. About a dozen of them!"

Clark smiled. "Sounds like Lex."

"This whole thing reminds me of that old David Lynch movie, *Blue Velvet,*" Shaaban said darkly. "I saw it in London. On the outside, there's this splendid little town, but underneath —"

"Smallville is a great town, Shaaban," Clark insisted.

"Strange," Chloe added, "but great."

"No sane person would send an oil truck at

someone's home," Dr. Mwariri insisted. "And I don't want you to start judging people harshly because one idiot vandalized our home, Shaaban."

Shaaban's eyes narrowed. "Come on, Dad. We can't feel safe any longer. It makes me wish we had never left Tanzania."

It hurt Clark's heart to hear his friend say that. "We're glad you're here, Shaaban," he said softly. "And we're not going to let anyone ruin Smallville."

"Maybe the truck thing really was just an accident," Tina said hopefully.

"Just to be on the safe side, Tina," Lana counseled, "I'd take the security."

Tina reluctantly agreed, and she left with Shaaban and Pete. Dr. Mwariri took off for a meeting at Luthorcorp. Chloe said that she'd go over to the farmhouse kitchen and raid the fridge. Which left Clark alone with Lana.

Not that I mind, Clark thought. He sneaked a look over at Lana, whose face was still flushed from dancing. *How is it that she always seems to shine from someplace deep inside of herself?*

"The African dance is fun, isn't it?" Lana asked.

"I'm assuming I don't look as dorky as I feel," Clark admitted.

"You're a very good dancer, Clark."

And I've danced with you so many times in my dreams. But I could never tell you that without looking like a fool.

He shrugged. "I'm okay."

She looked down at the floor as if she was studying something. "So . . . ," she finally began, "I hung around for a reason."

"To tell me how great my dance of Truth is?" he teased her.

"Frankly, it could use a little work."

Clark put his hands to his heart. "Ouch."

She chuckled. "Actually, I was hoping we could talk, Clark."

"Sure."

Her eyes flicked toward the stairs. "Maybe this isn't a good time. Chloe's coming back."

She wants to talk to me alone, Clark realized. *Excellent.*

"Maybe I could stop over later," Lana suggested. "Unless you already had plans."

"No, no plans," Clark quickly assured her, all

thoughts of checking out Dennis Jones's alibi flying from his brain. "Is everything okay?"

"That's kind of a wide-open question," she commented.

"I just meant that if anything is wrong, if there's anything I can do —"

"Hey Clark, shake a leg and give me a hand," Chloe called as she came up the loft steps with a tray of food. Lana and Clark both reddened, as if she'd caught them at something.

"Oh. Lana. I didn't realize you were still here." Chloe cocked her head to the side. "Am I interrupting?"

"Actually, I was just leaving," Lana assured her.

"I wasn't hinting," Chloe said. "If you want to come with us after we eat . . . ?"

Lana looked quizzically at Clark. "I thought you said you didn't have plans."

Clark reddened. "Uh, I guess I forgot."

Lana nodded. "No problem. I'll see you later."

Chloe watched Lana leave. "I ask you this in my capacity as an investigative journalist," she began. "What's the story with you and Lana?"

"What are you talking about?"

"Female intuition."

"There's nothing to investigate, Chloe."

"She said that she'd see you later," Chloe reminded him. "I took that literally. But if it's some big secret . . ."

"It's not a big anything. She said she might stop over, later. That's all."

"Oh."

"She just wants to talk to me, Chloe. Hold on while I write a note for my parents so they know where I am." He grabbed paper from the drawer near the phone and scribbled a quick note. "I'll leave this in the kitchen on the way out."

Chloe leaned over his shoulder to see what he was writing. "All I said was, 'Oh,' Clark."

Clark dead-eyed her. "It was a loaded 'oh.'"

"Oh."

Clark groaned.

"Besides," Chloe went on, all sweetness and light, "I'm sure if the two of you get engaged during your big talk tonight, I'll definitely be among the first to know."

CHAPTER 15

"**W**hat's really driving me nuts is how no one seems to know anything about the fire at the Hiromuras," Chloe told Clark as she pulled into the Luthorcorp subdivision. "I made a list of all the people who lived in Smallville during the fire in 1941 who still live here now." She nudged her chin toward her purse, which sat between them on the seat. "It's that piece of paper sticking out of the pocket."

Clark scanned the list. Most of the names were crossed off. "So everyone whose name you crossed off refused to talk to you?"

"Some of them talked. Most of those didn't even remember. The ones who did said it was an accident and they didn't know anything about it."

"Right at the next corner," Clark instructed Chloe, still looking at the list. "Hmmm. Who's Gilbert Melrose? Is he Deputy Melrose's father?"

"Grandfather. He's in that assisted living place on the road to Metropolis. Still perfectly lucid, as far as I can tell. So I asked him about the fire. He told me not to stick my nose where it didn't belong."

"That's odd."

"No kidding," Chloe agreed.

"Take the next left and go to the end of the block," Clark said. "We're looking for Twelve-twelve Forest Hills Lane."

"There it is," Chloe said, parking a bit up the street from Dennis's house. "So, big guy. What's your great plan?"

"Brian told me he had another tutoring session with Dennis at the library. And that Dennis's parents are picking them both up at nine P.M., after the movies. Which means, hopefully, that no one is home."

"I love a good case of breaking and entering," Chloe quipped.

"Maybe it won't be locked."

Clark felt a pang of guilt over what they were about to do, but the need for action was stronger. "If we wait around for Deputy Melrose to handle this, it could be next century. Melrose is still trying to investigate me."

"I see your point."

They approached the house. The sign on the front lawn was prominent: PROTECTED BY METROPOLIS ALARM COMPANY. ARMED RESPONSE.

"We'd better hope they left a door open," Chloe said.

They tried the front door. Locked. So was the back door. Clark looked up at the windows. Also locked.

What else? I don't want to leave a trace that I've been here. And I definitely don't need an armed response.

He looked around. Near one corner of the house was an entrance to a storm cellar, much like the one at the Kent farm. If he were lucky, there'd be a trap door from the storm cellar leading into the house. But the cellar entrance was bolted shut with a two-inch-thick metal chain.

He knew he could pop the chain with his super-strength, but only if Chloe wasn't watching.

I have to get rid of Chloe for a minute. Here goes nothing.

"Oh, man," Clark groaned, grabbing his stomach and doubling over.

"What?" Chloe looked alarmed.

"Cramps. Major. I got some kind of intestinal thing from my mom," he invented. "It just came on all of a sudden."

"We can come back another time —"

"Agrh," Clark said, bent like a pretzel. "I've got medicine. In my backpack. In your car." He crumpled to the grass and tried to moan convincingly.

"I'll go get it for you. Don't move."

"Thanks, Chloe."

As soon as Chloe was out of sight, Clark zipped over to the storm cellar. He grabbed the heavy chain in his hands and snapped it like a child's toy, then opened one of the doors and climbed inside.

Don't forget to fuse that chain back together later, he told himself.

Clark super-sped through the storm cellar, found

the trap door, and emerged in the house's actual basement. He saw laser beams crisscrossing the doorway, and knew that breaking any of them would set off the burglar alarm. So he had to crawl underneath their latticework, curling and spinning. Then, he hurried through the house until he found the master control switch in the living room. One hard tap from his right index finger and the system was completely disabled.

"Clark? Clark!"

He heard Chloe calling. He zoomed into the kitchen and opened the back door for her, motioning for her to hurry inside.

"How did you get in?" she demanded.

"Umm . . . basement window," he said evasively. "I checked, no one's here."

"What about your killer cramps?" She held out his backpack to him. For a moment, he couldn't figure out why.

Right! My "pills."

"I couldn't find any pills in there, Clark. But you seem to have made a miraculous recovery, anyway."

"Comes and goes, I guess," Clark said.

She didn't look convinced. "And what did you do about the security system?"

"Lucky break. They forgot to turn it on," Clark replied.

"You sure?"

Clark nodded. "Come on. Let's go check out Dennis's room."

"Lead the way."

They found the room easily enough. Posters for metal bands from the late-1970s lined the walls. There was a TV against one wall, and a videotape machine sat on top of it. Rows of tapes were stacked against one wall.

"I don't suppose a love for AC/DC makes him a criminal," Clark said.

"Only for the bad music police." Chloe roamed the room. "If we could only find a journal, something like that."

They looked around for a while, but found nothing incriminating.

"We'd better check the rest of the house," Clark said. "Don't want to be here if they come home early."

They looked around as much as they dared,

but found nothing. Their last stop was the attached garage. Clark opened the door.

"Uh-oh," Chloe gulped, when she saw what was inside.

The garage was obviously used for storage, not for sheltering parked cars. The floor was covered in oilcloths. Several large ladders were propped against one wall. Stacked in a corner were dozens and dozens of paint cans. And hanging on another wall were professional yard signs — poster boards stapled to wooden stakes:

TWO TEENS PAINTING SERVICE
New to Area: We Have Great Rates!
555-8756

Well, that could explain the spray paint in the locker, Clark thought to himself. There were several big cardboard boxes in the garage, and other stuff covered by more drop cloths. He idly started firing his X-ray vision at it all.

"Hey!" Chloe exclaimed. "Maybe since they have a painting business, it was easier for them to spray-paint Shaaban's —"

"Actually, I don't think so," Clark surmised. He went to one of the drop cloths and pulled it off a pile of stuff, having seen with his X-ray vision what was underneath. Now revealed were several concert-style music speakers, electric guitars in cases, and a full rock 'n' roll drum kit.

"A garage band," Chloe said. "In the garage."

Clark picked up a sheath of papers atop one of the speakers and looked at them. "Check this out, Chloe."

She peered around his arm. The papers were receipts for rehearsal time at a music studio in Metropolis. Clark shuffled through them, and then held up one of them.

"Here's their alibi. They were rehearsing in Metropolis when Shaaban's house was trashed. This is the receipt. Signed by both Dennis and Phil."

"Great," Chloe said. "We ended up finding an alibi instead of nailing them."

"I'm happy we were wrong," Clark told her. "Do you realize what we did? We suspected Dennis and Phil on the basis of their looks. How messed up is that, Chloe?"

"It was behavior, too," Chloe reminded Clark. "He and his bud didn't applaud at the assembly."

"We judged them without knowing all the facts," Clark said as he made another mental note to re-fuse the metal on the lock to the storm cellar.

Wouldn't want to forget that.

"Okay. We made a mistake." Chloe sighed. "So if it wasn't the dark dudes from Idaho, who's doing it?"

"I don't know, Chloe. We're right back where we started on this thing. But we'll figure it out."

She took a deep breath before she turned to face him again. "We have to, Clark. Because honest to God, I don't think I can keep living in this town unless we do."

Chapter 16

Clark aimed his telescope toward Lana's house and peered through the viewfinder, hoping to see her heading across the fields toward his loft, as she'd promised. But he didn't see her at all.

He sighed. Maybe it had been silly to count on her coming over. But he had it all worked out so perfectly. Shaaban had gone to the movies with his parents, so he had the loft to himself. The Dave Matthews Band was on the CD player. The night was full of stars and promise.

All I'm missing is the girl.

He took another peek through his telescope. Nothing.

"Utumaliza limau shaba haiwi dhahabu." Clark murmured a Swahili proverb that Shaaban had

taught him as he focused on Lana's house. Translated literally, it meant that copper would never turn to gold.

In other words, Clark thought, *don't wish for the impossible. And for me, Lana is the —*

"Clark?"

He whirled. Lana stood at the top of the stairs. Suddenly, he couldn't figure out where to put his hands. He settled for shoving them deep into the pockets of his jeans. "You came."

"I almost didn't," she admitted. "I walked the long way. That's why you didn't see me through your telescope."

"I wasn't looking for . . ." He stopped. It was such a stupid, obvious lie. "Busted," he admitted.

"Pardoned." She came to him and put her eye to the viewfinder, aiming the telescope up at the stars. "Do you ever wonder what's out there, Clark?"

More than you could possibly know.

"Sometimes."

"I'd like to believe that there really is life on other planets," she said wistfully. "It makes the world seem less lonely, somehow. Sometimes I look up at the moon and think about Whitney . . . how, at that very moment, he might be looking up at the very same moon."

Clark felt certain that she was trying to tell him that she finally realized how committed she was to her relationship with Whitney. So, that's what she'd wanted to tell him. Well, he'd have to accept it. He couldn't force her to love him.

But why does it have to hurt so much?

"I understand, Lana," Clark forced himself to say. "I'm sure he misses you just as much as you miss him."

Lana turned to Clark. "No, you don't understand. If I could deliver a message to that moon, it would be to tell Whitney that I'm not sure I'm in love with him at all. I can't let him live a lie, believing that I'm someone I'm not." She ran her hands impatiently through her hair. "God, I sound like such a drama queen."

"You know, you should wait until Whitney gets home to —"

"I know I should, Clark. I mean, I keep telling

myself that. But I feel like my life is on hold, and I hate it. It's exactly why I wouldn't commit to him before he left."

"I understand," Clark said.

"I don't. Not exactly, anyway," Lana admitted. "I can't find the right words. Maybe it would be easier like this."

Slowly, she raised her arms and turned her palms toward Clark.

For romantic love, the palms face inward, toward the beloved.

"Lana —"

"You don't have to say anything. I just need you to know why I couldn't send that tape to Whitney."

Clark went through an intense inner struggle. Nothing would make him happier than to pull Lana to him and kiss her right now the way he'd dreamt of kissing her. But how could he?

"You and Whitney were together a long time, Lana," he finally said. "And Whitney went through so much when his dad got sick . . ."

"Don't you think I know that?" Lana said

softly. "I'm not telling you I don't have any feelings for Whitney, because that would just be another lie. But I am telling you that . . . I have feelings for someone else, too. I'm not going to do anything about it. Not now. But I need to be honest with you. So you don't think less of me."

"That would never happen, Lana," Clark assured her. And then, slowly, he raised his own palms toward her.

She walked toward him, until — at last — her palms met his. "There's been so much hate in Smallville lately, Clark," she whispered. "It's good to know that there's love here, too."

CHAPTER 17

GENESIS DIARY, ENTRY #3

CAN'T SLEEP. CAN'T EAT. THE REDS
COME ON ME MORE AND MORE. I KNOW WHY.
IT'S BECAUSE I'M FAILING MY DAD.
LETTING HIM DOWN, AFTER HE TRUSTED
ME WITH THE HOURGLASS. NO WONDER HE
HASN'T COME BACK FOR ME.

I HAVE BEEN WASTING MY GIFT. WHAT
IF I HAVE A LIMIT ON THE NUMBER OF
TIMES I CAN RE-ENTER THE ZONE?
WHAT IF MY HOURGLASS SHOULD BE
STOLEN, OR SHATTERED? WHAT IF, WHAT
IF, WHAT IF? I NEED TO KEEP IT WITH
ME ALWAYS, JUST TO BE SAFE.

MY NEW PLAN IS TO BIDE MY TIME. ONE
MORE HIT, MAYBE. ON THE VIETNAMESE NAIL

SALON ON MAIN STREET. THEN, I'LL GIVE
SMALLVILLE A MULTICULTURAL FESTIVAL
IT WILL ALWAYS REMEMBER. BUT NOT
THE FESTIVAL ITSELF — IT WILL BE
CRAWLING WITH POLICE, I'M SURE. IN-
STEAD, THAT MORNING, THERE'S A SERVICE
AT THE CHURCH ON THE ROAD TO JASPAR.
THEY'LL ALL BE THERE. KENT, LANG,
ROSS, WU, EVEN THE FAMILY FROM
AFREAKA. BY THE TIME I'M DONE,
THERE'LL BE NO MULTICULTURAL PEOPLE
LEFT TO ATTEND THE FESTIVAL.

DAD, KNOW THIS: LIKE FATHER, LIKE SON.
BRIAN PARSON WAS THE ONE.

CHAPTER 18

The next afternoon, Clark and Chloe were in the backseat of the Kents' second car — Jonathan Kent driving, Martha Kent next to her husband — heading back to Smallville.

Clark leaned toward Chloe. "Maybe there are some sources we missed."

"There aren't," Chloe said. "I interviewed everyone. I even doubled back and called some of them again. I got nothing, Clark. Zip. Zero. Nada. There's no way to prove that the fire was arson."

Martha craned around in her seat. "I know how much it means to you to prove that the fire at the Hiromura place was no accident," she said. "But really, what will it accomplish? Hate has always existed, you know."

"That's why we need justice," Clark insisted, thinking about what he'd heard Lex say.

"And that's why we're not giving up," Chloe growled.

Jonathan glanced at her in his rearview mirror. "I do admire your spunk, Chloe. That's why I tracked down Sid and Mary Wilson, over in Jaspar. They were friends of my parents and used to live in Smallville. It's too bad they couldn't help you."

"I know," she said glumly, staring out the window at the passing cornfields.

Clark nudged her with his elbow. "Hey. I have something that might cheer you up."

"What?"

"I did some research on the computer last night. I think I actually found Joellen Hiromura."

Chloe's eyes grew wide. "You're kidding."

"Well, it's not a very common name. A woman with her name is living in San Francisco. She was a curator at the de Young Museum of art in Golden Gate Park, but she's retired now. So that means she's in the right age range. I really do think it's her."

"That's great, Clark. Why don't you two kids write to her?" Martha suggested.

"To say what?" Chloe asked. "We know someone deliberately burned your house down and wrecked your life, but too bad, we can't prove it?"

"We just haven't proved it *yet,*" Clark insisted.

"It is possible that you won't find what you're looking for, son," Jonathan said as he moved the car forward over a cattle guard.

"Whose side are you on, Dad?" Clark demanded.

"Whoa, hold on, Clark. I drove you to the Wilsons, didn't I? I know you're frustrated. But I'm not the enemy."

"Sorry," Clark mumbled. Irritated at his own impotence in this situation, he looked out the window. They were passing the cornfield where the Hiromura home used to be.

But it looked entirely different.

Chloe was slack-jawed. "What the heck is going on?"

What yesterday had been a bucolic cornfield was now a beehive of activity, with most of the crop trampled to the ground. Tractors, backhoes, and earth-moving equipment, all bearing the Luthorcorp logo, were digging into the soil. Meanwhile, in the center of the area, people were streaming in and out of a small trailer that appeared to be some kind of impromptu command post.

"Lex," Clark surmised.

"Care to explain?" Jonathan asked.

"I asked him for help."

Martha peered out her window. "Well, it would appear that you're getting what you asked for."

"Dad, can we stop?"

"I hope Lex has some kind of permit to do this," Jonathan remarked as he pulled the car off the road and onto a dirt path that had been cut through the flattened cornstalks. "Not that Lex Luthor would let a little thing like the law get in his way."

Jonathan pulled up by the mobile home just as Lex was stepping out of the trailer.

"Hello, all," Lex greeted them expansively. "Sorry I haven't gotten back to you, Clark. But as you can see, I'm providing the assistance you asked for."

"Which I appreciate," Clark said. "But this isn't your field. How can you be digging it up?"

"The timely and judicious application of capital and equipment to any problem can yield substantial results," Lex intoned, sweeping his hand over the land. "Hence, the active examination of a potential crime scene you see before you."

"The Luthors don't own Smallville," Jonathan told him. "People here do not take kindly to trespassers."

Lex smiled. "I so agree with you, Jonathan. Which is why I purchased the property on which you're now standing."

"Seriously?" Martha asked.

Lex smiled.

"Money talks, bull walks," Chloe put in. She watched people lugging plastic bags full of soil into the trailer. "I'm impressed."

Lex bowed his head toward her. "Thank you, Chloe. Always nice to be appreciated."

Clark cocked his head toward the trailer. "What's going on in there?"

"Mobile crime lab," Lex explained. "Know the right people, make the right calls. Some of the finest forensic scientists in the state have come to our aid. What we're looking for won't take —"

At that moment, a red-haired and white-coated scientist came out of the trailer, spotted Lex, and headed for them.

"Speaking of the finest forensic scientists," Lex said. "This is Dr. Mariah Berman. She's heading up the investigation."

Dr. Berman nodded distractedly and thrust a piece of paper at Lex. "It's absolutely confirmed. We've done a series of soil analyses from several feet below the initial layer of topsoil, adjacent to the foundation."

"Your conclusion?" Lex queried.

"As we suspected, there was residual ash from the fire, along with other nonsoil elements," Dr. Berman said. "Most importantly, we found incontrovertible proof of an accelerant."

"Excellent work, Dr. Berman."

"Wait a minute," Clark blurted excitedly. "You're saying that someone used a flammable substance to start the fire?"

"Not exactly. I'm saying that once the fire started, someone poured something on the building to make it burn more quickly." Dr. Berman impatiently pushed the red hair off her face. "In this case, it was gasoline. According to my chemical analysis, leaded gasoline."

"*Leaded gasoline?*" Jonathan asked. "But they haven't made leaded gas in years."

"Exactly, Dad," Clark said, his heart pounding. "It means we can eliminate the possibility that the accelerant got into the ground recently. It has to be connected to the fire!"

Dr. Berman smiled. "That's right, young man. What's your name?"

"Clark Kent."

"Perhaps you should consider a career in law enforcement, Clark," the scientist said.

"I've got bigger plans for Clark," Lex interjected.

Jonathan dead-eyed Lex. "So do I."

"So do I!" Chloe yelped. Everyone turned to her, puzzled. "Just felt like chiming in," she said with a sheepish grin.

"I'm hoping to plan my own future," Clark

said. "But at the moment, I'd rather concentrate on the present. Dr. Berman, is there any chance that this fire was accidental?"

She shook her head. "None."

"Is there any way to tell where the gasoline came from?" Martha asked.

"There's a remote chance that we might be able to figure out the brand," Dr. Berman said, "if the manufacturer used some kind of chemical tag in it. But it's a long shot."

"Well, then, try to do it," Lex ordered. "And anyone else in there that you need to help you, put them to work, too."

"I'll do that, Mr. Luthor. Nice to meet you people." She disappeared back inside the trailer.

"Thanks, Lex," Clark said. "For all of this."

Lex waved him off. "Anyone who cares about Smallville as much as I do would have done the same."

Chloe folded her arms. "So we were right all along, Clark. It really was arson."

Clark nodded. "But what we don't know is, who was the arsonist?"

"Figuring that out may prove to be impossible, Clark," Martha said. "The crime is more than sixty years old."

"In the existential scheme of things, that's barely a heartbeat," Lex pointed out. "I promise you that if it's possible, it will be done. No matter how long it takes, or how much it costs."

"Thanks, Lex," Clark said gratefully.

Lex clapped Clark on the back. "No need for thanks, Clark. All I'm doing is the right thing."

CHAPTER 19

Pete, Clark, and Shaaban lolled on the bleachers, along with twenty other guys who were in their Friday morning gym class. Mr. Ballister was filling in for the gym teacher, who'd received a call that his wife had gone into labor. The class was already scheduled to do various Olympic-style events.

"Running the hundred-meter dash first thing in the morning," Clark grumbled. "Whose bright idea was this?"

Pete chuckled. "Karmic justice for a guy who's always running late." He clapped Clark on the back. "You need to put on some speed, man."

"He putters around in the morning like he's in slow motion," Shaaban teased. "Maybe Clark needs vitamin supplements."

It was difficult for Clark not to laugh at that one. "I'm fine."

"Tell you what," Shaaban said. "If they catch the culprits who trashed my home and we move back, you can stay over whenever you like. After all, it's only a few short blocks from school."

"*When* they catch them," Pete corrected.

Brian Parson jogged by with some friends. He waved to Clark, who waved back.

"That boy is seriously pale," Pete said, noting Brian's bare arms and legs. "He must own stock in sunblock."

"But if you need a tutor, Pete, I hear he's your man," Shaaban said.

Pete narrowed his eyes at Mr. Ballister, who was on the field writing on a clipboard. "What I need is a history teacher who doesn't hate my guts."

Shaaban shrugged. "I have Ms. Levine, so I can't comment."

"Gather 'round, gentlemen," Mr. Ballister called, waving the guys over to the sawdust-filled long jump pit.

"Now the long jump, that is my long suit," Pete went on. "It rewards speed, so I am about to kick serious butt. If Ballister dogs me anyway, we'll know I'm right about the guy having issues. I'll try not to make you look too bad, Clark."

"Gee, you're a pal."

Clark glanced at the football goalposts a hundred yards away.

I could take off from right here and land on the cross-bar. Not only would that be a world record, it would probably be a galaxy record.

"Ross!" the impromptu gym teacher shouted out. "You're up first."

Pete pointed at Clark. "Remember what I said."

He jogged to the start of the runway, took a deep breath, and then sprinted to the take-off board — although short of stature, Pete was extremely fast. Running full tilt, he planted his right foot and leaped into space, soaring out over the sawdust pit until he landed feet-first.

"Eighteen feet, six inches for Ross," a spotter announced. The other guys in the class applauded and cheered him on.

"Good job, Ross," Ballister called. "Martinez, you're up!"

Pete rejoined Clark and Shaaban. "He seemed

to treat you fairly just now," Shaaban pointed out.

"Yeah," Pete admitted. "He did."

"Joaquin Martinez, seventeen feet, ten inches!" the spotter called, after the kid made his landing.

"Good effort, Martinez!" Mr. Ballister praised the last jumper.

"Why is Ballister being so nice?" Pete wondered. "I don't get it."

"Pete, maybe you want to think about not killing the messenger," Clark advised.

Pete eyed him. "What do you mean?"

"In my experience, Ballister is cool if he thinks you're doing your best . . . even if it isn't *the* best," Clark suggested. "Maybe he only rags on you in class because he knows how smart you are and thinks you could get A's. If you worked at it, that is."

"Maybe," Pete allowed reluctantly. "You know, Clark, I hate it when you're right."

"Kent, you're up!" Ballister shouted.

Clark jogged to the top of the runway. He wanted to do decently, but not so well that Ballister, or anyone else, would be impressed.

I definitely don't want them asking me to join the track team.

Ballister blew his whistle, and Clark started down the runway. He was careful to make a controlled — in his mind, puny — jump.

"Eighteen feet, five and fifteen-sixteenths of an inch!" the spotter called.

"Way to go, Kent!" Ballister called as Clark returned to the bleachers. "But so far, no one can touch Mr. Ross."

"I rule," Pete teased.

"Looks like you're right, Pete," Clark said, doing his best to be sheepish.

"So how about if you tutor Clark in the long jump, and he tutors you in history," Shaaban suggested.

Pete nodded. "Yeah, we might pull that off. You up for it, Clark?"

"Yeah, sure," Clark said. "It's a deal." He and Pete shared a fist-bump.

"Parson!" Ballister called.

Clark watched Brian, his pale skin gleaming even more brightly in the morning sunshine, hustle to the top of the runway.

Pete noticed, too. "Whoa," he said. "Maybe we

should buy him some of that fake suntan cream. He's so pale, I feel like I'm looking at a walking snowstorm."

Brian's long legs barreled down the runway. He jumped; his arms and legs windmilling as he struggled for every fraction of an inch.

"Eighteen feet, nine inches!" the spotter announced.

"Oh yeah!" Brian's fist pumped the air. The class hollered and applauded.

"Way to go!" Pete called to him, trying to be a good sport.

"Let it be known," Mr. Ballister said, checking his watch, "that at exactly nine o'clock, Mr. Parson established a new class record. You should go out for track, Brian."

"Yeah, cool. Maybe I will," Brian said. Flushed with victory, he joined his friends.

"Aw, I could take him if I trained," Pete mused. "He isn't all that that —"

Pete stopped mid-sentence. Clark was staring hard at Brian.

"What's up, big guy?" Pete asked.

"He made an excellent jump, but he's not worth *staring* at," Shaaban joked.

"Something's wrong," Clark muttered.

"Yeah, I'll tell you what's wrong," Pete said. "Brian beat me, you almost tied me, and Shaaban didn't even get his shot yet. Which means I need to spend a whole lot more time in the weight room."

"No. It's more than that." Clark couldn't take his eyes away from Brian.

Something's wrong. I know it is. I can't put my finger on it, but —

Clark's eyes widened as it came to him. "You guys," he hissed. "Check out Brian's legs."

"What about them?" Shaaban asked.

Clark's gaze was still focused on Brian. "And his arms. Unbelievable." He turned to his friends. "He's got a gauze bandage on his arm. And it's red around it, as if he has a burn. There's another one on his left leg."

Pete was bewildered. "So?"

Clark closed his eyes, trying to picture Brian just a few moments ago walking to the top of the runway for his broad jump.

Yes. I'm sure of it.

"Guys, those bandages weren't there when he started that jump."

Pete frowned. "Get out. They must have been there."

Shaaban nodded. "I agree. We just didn't notice them."

But Clark was certain. "I'm telling you, *they weren't there.*"

Pete shook his head. "What are you saying? That they just sort of magically appeared on Brian's skin?"

"Something like that."

Pete playfully hit himself in the forehead. "Of course. Why didn't I think of that? Brian's an alien from the planet Bandage."

Shaaban laughed. "Come on, Clark. You've told me that strange things sometimes happen in Smallville. But bandages out of nowhere?"

"I know it sounds crazy," Clark allowed, "but I'm sure —"

"Mwariri!" Mr. Ballister called.

Shaaban headed for the long jump runway,

and Pete clapped for him. "Okay, Shaaban. Let's see some *real* magic, big guy!"

❧ ❧ ❧ ❧

Clark, Pete, and Shaaban carried their trays out of the food service line and snaked through the crowded cafeteria to their usual spot, where they slid into some free seats. Clark took in the heaping pile of spaghetti on Pete's tray. "You must be hungry."

"Carbo loading." Pete swirled his fork in the spaghetti. "I'm serious about the gym thing. I'm going to break Brian's class record. Maybe those magic bandages gave him superstrength, or something."

Clark opened his carton of milk. "It's not funny, Pete. I just need to —"

"Big news," Chloe called, barreling over to them.

"Where's the fire?" Pete quipped, forking up more spaghetti.

"Downtown," Chloe reported, sliding into a seat. "And it's bad."

Pete looked incredulous. "Hey, I was kidding."

"I wish I was. You know the Vietnamese nail place on Main Street? Tran's place? Someone fire-bombed it this morning."

"Oh my dear God," Shaaban whispered. "It's another hate crime, I know it."

"Anyone hurt?" Clark asked quickly.

Chloe nodded. "Two of Tran's nail techs are in the hospital's burn unit. Tran was in the alley taking out the trash, or she'd probably be there, too."

"No customers?" Pete asked.

"It happened at nine and the place doesn't open until ten," Chloe explained. "Thank God for small favors, I guess."

Suddenly, Clark felt as if the puzzle pieces that had been swirling around in his mind were finally dropping into place. "What time did you say it happened, Chloe?"

"According to the fire department, the alarm went off at nine exactly. Why?"

"It's Brian," Clark declared.

"No way," Pete scoffed. "Brian was at school beating me in the long jump, dude."

"He made his jump at exactly nine o'clock," Clark said. "Mr. Ballister announced it, remember?"

"I am totally lost," Chloe confessed. "What does Brian Parson have to do with anything?"

"I think he's the guy we're looking for," Clark said.

One of Chloe's eyebrows headed north. "Brian Parson? The kid who tutors everyone? Whose mom is running the multicultural festival on Sunday? I don't *think* so."

"I'm serious," Clark insisted, his mind in overdrive. "I think that somehow he's able to get inside the fabric of time, do what he wants to do, and then reappear." He turned to Pete and Shaaban. "That's why he didn't have any bandages when he started his jump, but did when he finished. Because in between, he was firebombing Tran's place."

Chloe looked bewildered. "I feel like I walked in on the last act of a mystery."

Clark quickly explained what had happened during gym class that morning.

"You mean he's in two places at once?" Chloe asked. "Bi-locating?"

"No. I mean he's moving so quickly that essentially it's as if he can freeze time. He can move, but we can't."

"How is that possible?" Shaaban asked. "It sounds like science fiction."

"What it sounds like is a green meteorite effect," Chloe said slowly. "So the Mwariri attack, and the Wu attack, and —"

"Even the flyers Lana and I were putting up," Clark concluded. "I think he did it all."

Shaaban shook his head. "What you two are talking about is impossible."

"Not in Smallville," Pete informed him.

"Okay, even if it were possible, why would Brian do these things?"

"I don't know," Clark admitted.

"We need to go to the cops," Pete said.

"Puhlease," Chloe snorted. "We're going to tell Deputy Melrose that Brian Parson can create wormholes in time and uses this power to commit hate crimes?"

Pete nodded. "You're right. I believe it and I *still* don't believe it."

Shaaban looked at Clark. "So what do we do?"

"I don't know," Clark admitted. "But it's up to us to stop him from whatever he's planning to do next."

CHAPTER 20

"**S**peak of the devil," Pete said. He indicated with his chin toward the doors of the cafeteria, where Brian was entering with some friends.

"I'll go talk to him," Clark said, rising. Pete and Shaaban got up, too.

"We're with you," Shaaban assured him.

"Thanks, but I think I should approach him alone," Clark said. "Odds are, he'll be defensive. If three of us confront him, who knows what he'll do? Let me do it alone."

"What if he speeds into that fast time, though?" Chloe asked. "You'll be talking to him, all hell will break loose, and there won't be a thing you can do about it!"

That's not exactly accurate. Because I can go there, too. Clark time.

"I think I can handle him," Clark assured his friends.

"We'll be watching, in case you need us," Pete told him.

"Thanks." Clark turned and headed for the table where Brian was now seated with his friends. He moved slowly, concentrating hard, trying to figure out what he wanted to say.

He felt a hand on his arm and turned to see Lana, smiling up at him. "You're looking serious, Clark. It's so nice out. Want to go for a walk before class starts?"

Clark kept his eyes fixed on Brian. "I can't, Lana. Sorry. Excuse me." He knew he sounded curt, and he saw out of the corner of his eyes the hurt on her face. But he couldn't think about that now. He had a job to do.

He was almost to Brian's table when the wave of pain hit him. He staggered a little, but managed to stay upright by grabbing the edge of a table he was passing.

Meteorite pieces must be around here. But where?

Then Clark saw Brian extract an hourglass from his backpack, unwrapping its protective bubble wrap so he could show it off to his friends. There were glints of green amid the white sands of the hourglass, and Clark figured it out immediately.

There must be fragments of the green meteorites in the sand. It's deadly to me. But it must be the hourglass that gives Brian his power.

I can't let it stop me. I can't.

Clark gritted his teeth and pulled down his sleeves. He didn't want anyone to see his veins bulging and crawling, black under his skin, a sure sign of exposure to the meteorites. Willing himself forward, he shuffled across the linoleum, feeling as if someone were twisting his spinal column into a double helix.

Can't stop. Have to persuade him to turn himself in.

"Brian?" he gasped. "Can I talk to you?"

"Hey, Clark. Are you okay, buddy? You look sick."

"I'm . . . fine. Can we talk? Privately?"

Brian shrugged to his friends. "Sure thing," he told Clark with a smile. "Have a seat."

Even in Clark's weakened state, a Swahili proverb he'd learned from Shaaban flew into his mind: *Machoni rafiki, moyoni mnafiki. Friendly in the eyes, a hypocrite in the heart.*

Black spots swam before Clark's eyes. "Talk . . . outside? Important."

"Sure," Brian said easily. But Clark saw wariness flicker in Brian's eyes, and a muscle jump in his cheek.

He knows, Clark realized. *And he knows I know. What am I going to do? I feel so weak.*

Suddenly, Brian flipped the hourglass. The green-flecked sand oozed downward. With its movement, a new wave of agony washed over Clark. His knees buckled, and he barely caught the edge of the table.

"I mean it, Clark. You look terrible," Brian observed. "I'm walking you down to the nurse's station."

With that, Brian took two steps toward Clark and then a giant leap.

He's going into the warp . . . I can't let him escape!

With an animal howl, Clark used his last ounce of strength to leap away from the table and its deadly hourglass. And then, he put on a burst of superspeed, moving so quickly into Clark time that the cafeteria looked frozen — people's forks held to open mouths, the doors open with students coming inside, others in mid-conversation with arms looking silly in mid-gesticulation.

He swung his head this way and that, looking.

Where's Brian?

Suddenly, Clark felt himself hurled into a high rack of freshly washed dishes and glasses. They came smashing down all around him. Clark lifted the rack off his chest and tossed it aside.

There was Brian, standing twenty feet away.

"How did you get here, Clark?" Brian demanded. "You don't belong here!"

"You're the one who doesn't belong here. I know what you did, Brian. You need help."

"You think *I* need help?" Brian laughed until spittle flew from his mouth like pellets from a shotgun. "I'm the savior of Smallville, you idiot."

"No, Brian. You're not."

"I took you for someone with half a brain, Clark. I should have known better." He pointed at Pete and Shaaban, who were seemingly frozen at their table. "You hang out with all the Others. The ones who don't belong here."

"You're a disturbed person."

"No. Someone really sick would have hurt the Africans or killed the Wus. I just tried to get them to leave."

Clark controlled the anger within himself. "You firebombed the nail salon, Brian. People are in the hospital!"

"Because no one is getting the *message!*" Brian's voice rose and his eyes glittered unnaturally. "The Africans didn't leave. The Asians didn't leave. I didn't have any choice!"

"Why are you doing this?"

Brian looked at Clark curiously. "You don't get it? I'm using my power to fix things. You know. Back to the good old days."

"Whatever it is you think you're doing, I'm not letting you do it anymore."

"You can't stop me," Brian said with a shrug. "I will succeed. And when I do, my dad is coming back for me."

Maybe if I keep him talking . . .

"Where's your dad, Brian?"

Brian's eyes grew stormy. "No one will tell me. But he sends me things. He sent me the hourglass."

"Why don't we go back into real time," Clark suggested, slowly moving toward Brian. "I'll help you find him."

"Sure you will," Brian sneered. He pulled something from his jeans — a knife that glinted in the fluorescent light of the cafeteria.

"Brian, what are you —"

"Shut up!" Brian screamed savagely. At the same moment he pivoted, grabbed Lana, and put the knife to her throat.

"Don't hurt her!"

"Get out of my Zone," Brian said, his voice low and menacing. "You just want to ruin everything, and I won't let you."

Seeing the knife poised by Lana's flesh, Clark was filled with horror. He held his palms up to Brian. "Easy, guy. Just tell me what you want and I'll do it."

"Get out of my world," Brian snarled.

"Okay. I'm leaving. See?" Clark slowly backed away from Brian, weaving around frozen bodies. "I don't think you want to hurt Lana. I'm going to do exactly what you told me to do." Clark was fifty feet away, now. "Just lower the knife, Brian. Easy, now."

Brian's arm began to relax. The instant Clark saw that, he made his move.

Please, God. Let this be the right thing to do.

He didn't dive for Lana. Instead, he dove at the table on which the hourglass sat, screaming with agony as he slammed into it. The impact made the hourglass tumble and spin through the air.

"Nooooo!" Brian screamed, rushing for his treasure.

But it was too late. The hourglass hit the wall and shattered, its sand and green crystalline dust flying everywhere. Including directly at Clark.

"Argh!" Clark screamed as particles of deadly green sand drifted down on him. The sensation was just like the awful dream he'd had the night after the attack on Shaaban's home — when he'd felt green flames searing his skin. Even as Clark tried to brush the sand from his hair, he felt all the air punched from his lungs. He crumpled, as helpless as a toddler.

"How could you do that?" Brian cried. "It's from my dad!" Unhinged with fury, he threw the knife at Clark, missing by inches.

Clark, prone on the floor, looked around at the weird tableau of the cafeteria. He was stunned. He'd expected that shattering the hourglass would snap Brian back to the real world. But it hadn't. Everything and everyone still looked frozen. And now, Brian stood over him menacingly, a folding chair in his hands.

But even in his desperate, weakened state, Clark realized that at least Brian was no longer an immediate threat to Lana.

"I . . . need . . . to . . ." Clark huffed, too weak even to form a sentence.

"What do you need, jerk? This?" Brian lifted the chair high and then, with all his might, smashed it at Clark's stomach. The impact reverberated through the room, and Clark cried out in pain.

"Stop, Brian." Clark's words came out as a weak whisper.

But Brian didn't stop. He kept swinging the chair, and Clark writhed pitifully on the floor this way and that in a futile attempt to dodge the cascade of blows. "You've trapped me!" Brian shouted. "Trapped me, trapped me, trapped me! I'll never get out of here!"

One terrific blow from the chair hit Clark on the shoulder. But rather than hurt, it actually made Clark feel a tiny bit better. Clark quickly understood why: The breeze from the chair had blown some of the deadly meteorite particles out of his hair.

Those particles are all over the cafeteria. Like spores. I've got to get away, he thought frantically, trying to crawl toward the doors.

"Leaving so soon, Clark?" Brian asked sarcastically. "Go! It'll give me time to finish off your friends!" He let a terrific swing of the chair fly at Clark, smashing him out the cafeteria door. Then he turned with malice in his eyes toward Pete, Shaaban, and Tina.

Outside the cafeteria, Clark brushed the remaining particles from his head, and then knew exactly what to do. He super-sped down the hallway to where Dennis's and Phil's lockers stood, and ripped the entire bank of locker doors from the wall — a twenty-foot-long, five-foot-high, thin barrier of lead-painted metal.

The lead paint will shield me from the meteorite dust, Clark thought as he ran back to the cafeteria. He got there just as Brian was about to put a chokehold on Shaaban.

"Give it up, Brian!" Clark shouted as he approached the boy. The lead-painted, improvised metal shield was working perfectly — Clark felt fine.

"You're back?" Brian challenged. "I don't care. You can't stop me!"

"Oh yes, I can," Clark countered. With a super swing of his own, he whipped the improvised shield up and then down, unleashing a maelstrom of wind. Not only did the gust blow all the meteorite dust to the far end of the cafeteria, it whipped everything in the cafeteria that wasn't tied down — papers, books, and food — in the same direction.

Brian himself was knocked off-balance by the blast of air, and dropped to one knee. Clark was on him in a millisecond, throwing him backward thirty feet, away from his friends and against the cafeteria doors. Brian crashed hard into the double doors and slumped to the ground, barely conscious.

That's it for Brian, Clark thought. *It's over.*

He looked at the table where his friends sat, like figures in a wax museum, and knew he could return to the real world of his friends and family anytime he wanted. All he had to do was slow down enough to step out of Clark time.

But what about Brian? Would he be trapped in this limbo forever?

It was as if Brian was reading his mind. "Clark, you've got to help me," Brian whimpered. "Without the hourglass, I'll be stuck here!"

Suddenly, Clark got an idea — how to bring Brian back to reality and bring him to justice at the same time. He went over to a girl who'd been writing in a notebook. He plucked the pen from her rigid fingers and tossed it along with the notebook to Brian.

"I can help you," Clark said. "But *mchimba kisima huingia mwnyewe.*"

"What's that gobbledygook?" Brian demanded.

"It's a proverb in Swahili. Shaaban taught it to me," Clark said. "It means, 'he who digs a well gets himself inside.' And right now, Brian, I'd say you've dug yourself into one serious well."

"What do you mean?"

"It means I'm your only way back. Which is why you're going to find some paper, write a confession of all the terrible crimes you committed this week, and then give it to me," Clark told him.

"Like hell I will."

Clark shrugged. "Fine. Don't do it. You wanted to get rid of all the people who aren't like you? Well, congratulations. You got rid of *everybody*. Have a nice forever, all by yourself." Clark turned and began to walk away.

"Wait! You mean you'd leave me here?"

Clark turned back to him. "Unless you confess, yes."

"My dad left me," Brian said softly. "It's the worst thing in the world, to be all alone."

"Then write."

Clark waited while Brian wrote out a full confession. Then he insisted that Brian sign and date it.

"And add, 'I make this statement of my own free will,'" Clark instructed. Brian finished and handed the paper to Clark. "Now what?"

"Now, we give this to Principal Reynolds, who I see in the hallway outside the cafeteria. And then, I have an errand to do. And then, I'm going to take you back."

I hope.

Clark blindfolded Brian, strode out to the principal, and put Brian's confession in his frozen hand. Then he grabbed the metal locker doors, took them back down the hallway, and superfused them back in place.

And finally, he took Brian in his arms.

"What the —"

"Here goes," Clark told him. "Hold on."

Clark started to run, faster than he ever had before, around and around the cafeteria, a blur against the blur of time. Then, at maximum speed, he closed his eyes and jammed his feet to a dead stop.

He opened his eyes. He was standing in the center of the cafeteria, holding Brian in his arms. He dumped the blindfolded kid unceremoniously at his feet.

"Let go of me!" Brian screeched, pulling off the blindfold. "I mean it! I'll make you sorry!"

They were back in the real world. Kids rushed over, everyone talking at once. Time had returned to normal, as Clark had hoped.

Chloe gasped. "How'd you do that, Clark? And why is the cafeteria totally trashed?"

"I guess Brian isn't quite as speedy as he thinks," Clark said evasively. "And I guess he did a little damage while he was away."

The cafeteria lady ran out from behind a steam table. "Who broke my dishes?" she bellowed.

"Brian Parson!" the principal thundered, brandishing Brian's confession as he made his way through the crowd. "Don't let that boy get away."

"We won't!" Pete shouted. He and Shaaban went to Brian and pinned his arms behind his back.

Reynolds took out his walkie-talkie. "Have the Smallville sheriff's department send a team to the cafeteria," he ordered. "Right away." He turned to the crowd. "Back up, people. No one's putting on a show here."

Clark started to back away with everyone else, until Brian called to him. "Clark?"

Clark knelt down. "Yes?"

"Am I going to prison?"

"It's not up to me."

"I'm scared," Brian said quietly.

In spite of everything terrible that Brian had done, when Clark looked into his eyes, he saw a wounded boy looking back — a boy still capable of redemption.

"Wherever you go, you won't be alone, Brian." Clark put a comforting hand on Brian's shoulder. "I meant what I said before. You need help. I hope you get it."

EPILOGUE

The Multicultural Day festival was in full swing, the gym packed to the rafters with revelers. With the hate crimes of the past week solved, it seemed as if the whole town had come out to celebrate. Flags of various nations flew over the booths set up around the perimeter of the room, with the largest flag of all, an American flag, proudly mounted over the stage.

At the Mexico booth, little kids were swinging at a colorful piñata with long sticks. A small crowd at the Greece booth was learning to make stuffed grape leaves. At the booth for Russia, a Russian boy was teaching a group of children how to say "hello," "good-bye," and "that's so cool!" in Russian. And at the booth for Singapore, Tina's grandmother had a group enthralled with ancient Asian folktales.

The Mwariris, the Kents, Pete, Tina, Chloe, and Lana sat on a blanket at the Tanzania booth, enjoying the noontime feast Mrs. Mwariri had prepared. "Now this was worth waiting for," Pete said, shoveling another mouthful of ugali and spicy vegetable stew into his mouth.

"You should open a Tanzanian restaurant on Main Street, Mrs. Mwariri," Tina suggested. She helped herself to more ugali. "You'd make a mint."

Mrs. Mwariri nodded gracefully. "Food tastes better when it is made only for friends. But I thank you all for the compliments. I am so happy to be back in my own home, able to cook in my own kitchen."

"I still don't know how you figured out that it was Brian Parson, Clark," Tina said.

"Oh, he kind of gave himself away," Clark said easily.

"One moment I'm watching the dude unwrap his hourglass in the cafeteria," Pete began, "the next you've got him busted by Principal Reynolds. What's up with that?"

"It all happened kind of fast," Clark said, taking another bite of stew.

Chloe wagged a finger at him. "Like I always say, there's more to you than meets the eye, Clark Kent."

"What do you think will happen to him now, Clark?" Shaaban asked.

Clark shrugged. "I'm not sure. I understand he's at Arkum Asylum. There's a juvenile psych facility there. Maybe they can help him."

"I'd like to believe that Brian did what he did because he's ill," Lana said. "Not because he's really full of hate."

"Hate is something you learn," Martha said. "He definitely didn't learn it from his mother. Marilyn Parson is a good woman. She told me that Brian never really recovered when his dad ran off."

"That stinks," Tina pronounced.

"Yeah." Pete ate the last of his ugali. "But it's no excuse."

"Okay, I have to say this because it's driving me nuts," Chloe announced. "Brian thought he knew what was true about people when he didn't even know anything about them. Well, when it came to Dennis and Phil, I did the same thing. I mean, I think of myself as this tolerant and inclusive person, but I'm just as guilty of judging people as they are."

"So am I," Pete admitted. "Deputy Melrose, Mr. Ballister . . ."

"Don't be too harsh on yourselves," Mrs. Mwariri advised. "It's animal nature to be suspicious of those not like you. You should see how zebras act with other zebras on the savannah. If they're not in the same herd, they hate each other."

"We're not zebras, though," Dr. Mwariri pointed out. "Which is why the lesson you young people learned is one you will keep with you for your entire lives. The truth of a person can't be known until one takes the time to really know him."

The truth of a person can't be known until one takes the time to really know him. If people knew the truth about me, Clark thought, *a lot of them would be afraid, and they'd want me to go back where I came from. And I don't even know where that is.*

That thought made his throat dry. He excused himself to go to the water cooler in the hallway. When he got near the water cooler, he heard his name.

"Clark?"

He turned around. It was his mom.

"Are you okay?" she asked him.

"I was just thinking, Mom. Brian seemed so 'normal' that everyone thought they knew the truth about him. And I was thinking about how I seem 'normal,' too."

"People *do* know the truth about you," Martha insisted. "That you're good and kind and caring. People aren't defined by where they're from, Clark. They're defined by their actions."

She went to her son and took his hand. "And most of all, by what's inside their hearts." She smiled. "Come on, let's go back inside."

Together, they walked back to the gym, where a group of students singing an Italian folk song finished to a warm round of applause. Tina went to the mike.

"Thank you," she said, and consulted her clipboard. "That performance was organized by Rafaella Platini, whose family moved from Rome to Smallville when she was a young girl. I just want to remind everyone that a multicultural quilt is being assembled in the art room in the high school. After the quilt is assembled, it will tour our state, courtesy of Luthorcorp."

Tina continued at the microphone as Clark disappeared behind some sheets that cordoned off a makeshift dressing room area.

Clever, how Lex manages to do so much good and promote his company at the same time, Clark thought.

"Clark!" Shaaban waved Clark over to the small group who would soon be on stage doing their African dance. "Just in time. Here's your dashiki."

Clark took off his shirt and slipped the colorful tunic over his head. Then he admired Chloe and Lana, who were wearing *kanga* dresses they'd borrowed from Mrs. Mwariri. "You two look beautiful."

"You cut quite the dashing figure yourself," Chloe said.

Lana picked up something from a long table, turned around, and aimed a video camera at Clark. "So, Clark. How do you feel about the dance we're about to do?" she asked. "The dance of Truth?"

Is she making that tape for Whitney?

"I think Shaaban's got guts to be on the same stage as me," Clark told the camera. "I'll try not to knock him over."

Chloe popped her head in front of Clark and waved at the camera. "Hi, Whitney!" She blew a kiss at the lens.

Well, that answers that.

As Tina introduced the next performers, Clark talked and laughed with his friends. But he couldn't help watching, out of the corner of his eye, as Lana made her videotape.

A few moments later, she was tapping him on the shoulder.

"Lana, I don't really want to —"

"No camera." She'd put it down.

"You decided to send Whitney a new tape, huh?" Clark asked.

She nodded. "I decided it was ridiculous not to send one to him just because I'm not sure about our relationship. But there's no personal message." She smoothed a hank of her hair that didn't need smoothing. "Learning the truth about these hate crimes, past *and* present, really got me thinking. About what's real, and who I care about."

"You care about Whitney."

Her eyes searched his. "Whatever else is true, or not true, he and I have something special."

"That's good, Lana," Clark said. He knew they were the right words, but a part of him ached to say them.

"You guys, we're on in, like, two seconds!" Tina called out as she frantically wrapped her kanga on over her clothes.

"Who's going to introduce us?" Lana asked.

"Lex," Tina said with a shrug. "He insisted."

Lex's voice came over the sound system. "Ladies and gentlemen and children of all nations," his voice boomed. "I'd like to introduce the final act in Smallville High's presentation of performance art from around the world. Following this performance, there will be a special announcement."

"What's he talking about?" Chloe asked. No one, including Clark, had a clue.

"Now, representing Tanzania and the entire region of East Africa," Lex continued, "it is my honor to introduce Shaaban Mwariri, Tina Wu, Pete Ross, Chloe Sullivan, Lana Lang, and Clark Kent, with my good friend Dr. Donneth Mwariri on percussion, performing the dance of Truth."

"Let's get out there and show our stuff!" Tina whispered loudly, pushing the group out onto the stage. The seven of them faced a sea of people, which was amazing enough. But what was even more amazing was that everyone was waving solidarity flags.

Clark glanced over at Dr. Mwariri, who had taken his place behind the big drum. There were tears in his eyes.

Dr. Mwariri began a steady beating on his drum. The group swayed to the rhythm. As the drumming became more complex, they added the footwork and hand movements that Dr.

Mwariri had taught them, forming a circle and dancing toward each other. The movements represented the coming together of the village, all palms faced outward, then inward, pulsing to the beat.

Before they turned outward to dance back toward the audience, Clark felt Lana's hand on his heart. For the briefest instant, he covered it with his own. Then, Dr. Mwariri brought the drumming to a syncopated crescendo and the group spread out across the stage, finishing with palms outward — a sign that they were all part of the same community.

The crowd applauded, yelled "Bravo," and waved their flags, especially when Dr. Mwariri took a bow.

"I could get into this," Pete told Clark as they basked in the adoration. "I may have found myself a whole new career path."

The applause continued. The performers took another bow, then gestured toward Dr. Mwariri and joined in the ovation.

As the dancers left the stage, Lex stopped

Clark. "I'd appreciate it if you'd stay up here, Clark. You are about to escort someone very important to the microphone, my friend."

Clark had no idea what was going on, but did as Lex asked, waiting near the steps that led up to the stage.

Lex went back to the microphone, waiting for the crowd to quiet. "My friends, Smallville has experienced some trying times in recent days. But as I look out at this huge turnout and the flags you chose to carry, I know you feel the same way that I feel: that our differences, as well as our similarities, must be respected and celebrated. That's what we're doing here today."

The crowd roared its agreement.

"More than sixty years ago," Lex continued, "a terrible wrong was done to a Smallville family, simply because it was different. One week after Pearl Harbor, the home of Yoshi Hiromura was burned to the ground. Everyone thought it was an accident. But my recent investigation — sparked by the determination of Clark Kent and Chloe Sullivan — has proven that it was arson. The crime is still unsolved, but one can safely conclude that the family was burned out because of hate. Hate, my friends, is something we should never tolerate."

Near the front of the crowd, Clark saw his parents holding hands; his dad was gazing at Lex with something resembling respect.

"Sadly, Yoshi Hiromura and his wife died before we were able to uncover the truth of the wrong that was done to them. However, their daughter, Joellen Hiromura, who was only eighteen when her home burned down, is alive and well, living in San Francisco."

The crowd buzzed. This was exciting news. But not as momentous as what followed.

"With the assistance of Clark Kent, who recently located her, I was able to contact Ms. Hiromura," Lex went on. "And I invited her to be with us on this very special day."

Lex lifted his chin beyond Clark, who turned to see an elderly Asian woman with a shock of white hair just a few feet from him.

Lex never fails to amaze me, Clark thought as Ms. Hiromura took his arm. He escorted her up the steps and over to Lex, and the crowd cheered.

"Thank you, young man," Ms. Hiromura whispered. "Mr. Luthor told me that you're the one who uncovered the truth about the arson. It means a great deal to me."

When they reached Lex, he put his arm around Clark and invited Chloe to come to the stage as well. "Ladies and gentleman, were it not for Clark Kent and Chloe Sullivan, we would not have uncovered the truth. Ms. Hiromura has told me that her parents' dream was for her to graduate from Smallville High. At this time, I'd like to ask my friend Clark Kent to present Ms. Hiromura with her honorary diploma of graduation."

Lex bent down, took a framed diploma from under the lectern, and handed it to Clark as cheers again filled the gym. Clark held up both hands, pleading for the audience to quiet enough so that he could speak.

"Ms. Hiromura," Clark declared, "on behalf of the people of Smallville, we offer our most sincere apology for the wrong done to your family. I wish we'd been able to learn who the arsonist was. Maybe someday we will."

Ms. Hiromura nodded vigorously.

"I guess it's true," Clark continued, "that there's hate everywhere. But this town is full of good people, and the love here is a lot stronger than the hate. So, on behalf of us all, I hope you'll accept this honorary diploma from Smallville High School."

The crowd cheered and waved their flags as Clark handed the framed diploma to Ms. Hiromura. There were tears in her eyes and in those of so many people watching. Lex lowered the mike for the petite woman so she could say a few words.

"Thank you, Clark Kent." Her soft voice echoed through the gymnasium. "And thank you, Mr. Luthor. I have wonderful memories of Smallville that the terrible fire could never erase. And now I have wonderful new memories of Smallville, too. On behalf of my family, I thank you."

Now, the crowd stood as one and applauded until hands were hurting. Finally, Clark and Lex helped Ms. Hiromura down from the stage. Well-wishers immediately surrounded her.

Clark grinned at Lex. "How'd you pull this off?"

"I flew Ms. Hiromura here in the company jet. I think she deserves the best, don't you?"

"Absolutely. I don't know how to thank you for everything you've done, Lex. Buying the property, hiring the investigators, getting her here . . ."

"No need for thanks, Clark. The only difference between us is that when I choose to fight, I have the fiscal fortitude to back up my words."

Clark smiled inwardly. *If only Lex knew the powers I have when I choose to fight.*

"By the way," Lex continued, "I'm planning to deed the property back over to Ms. Hiromura. I'll tell her later; I didn't want to step on the moment."

"All I can say is, if you ever decide to run for president, Lex, count on me to be your campaign manager."

"I'll hold you to that, Clark. Excuse me. Duty calls." Lex edged his way back to Ms. Hiromura's side.

Clark watched hundreds of people — each one part of the tapestry that was Smallville at its best — line up to shake Ms. Hiromura's hand. Her face shone with joy.

Truth and justice, Clark thought. *Each of them is good. But when they come together like this, it's great.*

At that moment, Clark's friends pulled him into the happy throng. Clark went with them gladly, knowing that — no matter what — he was a part of the tapestry of Smallville, too. Now, and forever.

About the Authors

Cherie Bennett and Jeff Gottesfeld are a well-known writing couple, authors of several award-winning novels for young adults. Cherie is also one of the nation's leading playwrights for teens, a two-time winner of the Kennedy Center's New Visions/New Voices Award. As part of the inaugural writing staff for *Smallville*, the pair wrote the episode "Jitters." They answer all their email personally at authorchik@aol.com; learn more about them at their Web site, www.cheriebennett.com.